Stories by

Anna Krivolapova

Incurable

Graphomania

THIS IS AN APOCALYPSE CONFIDENTIAL BOOK
PUBLISHED BY APOCALYPSE CONFIDENTIAL PRESS
www.apocalypse-confidential.com

First Printing, September 2023

Our acknowledgment to Hobart, in which *Jersey Devil's Breath* first appeared.

Book design by Will Waltz.

Cover design by Mark Wadley.

ISBN 979-8-9873662-2-6

To N.N.K.

Contents

First Person Shooter

I DESERVE one good bender, I think.

I call an ex as I walk through the King of Prussia Mall looking for a bikini and new clothes.

"Meet me in Cape May tonight."
"Can't."
"Why, your parents at the house? We'll stay at mine, it's always empty."
"They're hunting."

Brett always says his parents are off hunting somewhere in the Pine Barrens or West Virginia. It sounds like a lie. My guess? They're in rehab, or that nude swinger resort in Berkeley Springs.

"Sounds like you can't talk right now."
"That's right. See you at work, Riley."

Brett milks my neutered name whenever his wife is in the room. There's some kind of Kuleshov effect happening. *Riley's* sexless cable knit Waspy qualities evaporate on the boot of a fictional Mercer County steelworker who wears it better. I want to go to the Piercing Pagoda and make the Romanian girl holding the gun give me therapy. I would let her riddle me with holes if she'd let me tell her about how I came home to a typed letter from my fiancé saying something along the lines of *I got a girl pregnant, it's over, you have one month to move out.*

"It didn't hit me while I was clearing out the apartment, renting a storage unit, or quitting my job. It hit me while I was parked in front of Wawa looking at photos of their shotgun wedding. She wore a sari to the courthouse. There was jewelry coming out of her nose and a red dot on her forehead."

"X marks the spot." The Romanian holds the piercing gun between my eyebrows. "But if you're going to the beach, you shouldn't get a new piercing. It could get infec—"

I walk away before she starts on infections or pus or anything that could bum me out. I go into Victoria's Secret and let the lady with measuring tape around her neck slide her hands around my ribs. It feels nice. She smells like tuberose and baby powder and feels sorry for me. She gives me a pink striped card with my name and bra size on it. *Riley, 32c.* My new business card.

I drive across the Whitman Bridge with my pink shopping bags riding shotgun. South Jersey's open farms, devilish woods, and pine-ringed swamps make my head spin. The air smells so good downwind of the Pine Barrens, where honeysuckle and chicory grow lush on the side of the highway. Nothing like the sulfur-ammonia bouquet I was living in. It's getting dark and half the cows are sitting down. Rain, maybe. I stop at Heritage Dairy for a cookies and cream milkshake. They call it the Holstein Shake after the black and white cows. The eternal schema for all cows. I wish they were all Holsteins. The brown cows remind me of India, of corpses floating through the Ganges and Graham's new wife.

There's no reception on Route 47 and I turn on FM radio. Beach Boys, Eagles, Alan Parsons Project, Creed, and Don Henley ride with me on the last stretch to Exit Zero. The DJ keeps dimming the volume to sing over the songs with his own mid-Atlantic interpretation of the lyrics. He sounds tanked.

I look for a place to park down the block after I finish unloading. The roads here are narrow and very few of the Victorian houses have driveways. The code to the lockbox is still grandpa's birth year. A smart thief would drive out here in April and try every house's lockbox starting with 1-9-2-0. I walk around the first floor using my phone as a flashlight before shutting the curtains and pushing the kitchen's dimmer up a centimeter.

I don't throw all the lights on like a madwoman. One lamp at a time. Sometimes, the smallest bit of candlelight is just enough. My grandmother was paranoid about electrical fires. She'd walk around the house with her nose in the air, hallucinating burnt plastic. She'd unplug the refrigerator at night and spoil the food. *I can hear it,* she contested. *I can hear it trying to burn the house down. It's cold, quiet, and wants to burn us alive.* I always thought there was something to it. She dislocated my shoulder a time or two when I was really small but they always clicked it back into place at Cape Regional. I always took her advice. She told me to buy a gray sedan, dark and nondescript, and to keep it clean with a trunkful of emergency. She was dying when she told me about the pink motel. She could have told me sooner. Every woman needs a break now and then.

The warm yellow light makes this house look just like it did 10, 20 years ago, when I ran through it with tiny sandy feet. It still smells like old wood, upholstery, and Grandpa. They never ended up renovating this place after he died. I usually sleep on the couch because the house gives me a haunted feeling that gets worse the higher up I go. The second and third floors scare me at night.

The mildew smell is overpowering and I go get the tent I keep in my trunk. The night is foggy and silent and every single house I pass is familiar to me. I start to feel hopeful. I pop the tent open in the middle of the living room carpet and crawl inside to sleep.

Tents make me feel safe and swaddled but I always wake up with an ache in my shoulders and lower back. I carry my bags to the third floor in the morning. I rush through the second floor— past my grandparent's bedroom, the pink bathroom with the big scale, and the two frilly bedrooms with one window each. On the third floor, everything is decorated with pale green and white accents. One of the closets opens to a staircase up to the widow's walk.

As a 7-year old, I desperately wanted a picture of myself in the widow's walk dressed up like Rapunzel. My grandpa tried, walking out into the front yard, crossing the street backwards until he hit the sidewalk, but there were too many trees obscuring me. The dense foliage surrounding the widow's walk makes it feel like a sanctuary, a princess' invisible tower. I can sit here and watch the street, the hotel, the boardwalk, and the ocean, all framed by Victorian gingerbread woodwork that costs a fortune to repair. One of the windows facing Megan's and the hotel has been broken since I was a child. The neighbors can't see the damage behind our sycamore tree so no one's bothered to fix it.

There's a key to the wine cellar somewhere on this ring. I try every one— the oldest looking one first. Not it. It's old and big and heavy with variegated teeth like a family photo. The cellar door is outside in the alleyway, parallel to the ground. If left open, an easy way for a child to get hurt. That mistake has caused some expensive hospital visits and big fights. The door unlocks stiff and crisp like it hasn't been touched in years. It opens up to dust and bikes and bags of charcoal. The wooden wine rack has been rotting down here, stone cold forgotten by everyone but the ocean air. I pick out three reds and crawl back upstairs. I try not to clink the glass bottles against our stone walkway and lay them on the budding tulips. Don't want to rouse the neighbors. There are six bottle openers in this house and they all have a tiny layer of rust. Every salt shaker is compacted with moisture.

Headlights sweep across the first floor. A Tahoe parks across the street, full of kids who sound tired but excited. I like how the insects start to get loud again this time of year; I miss them all winter long. They add a texture, a fuzz, a volume to the night. I enjoy the sounds of bugs and kids from my favorite bedroom in the house. Two walls of shelves fragrant with the signature lignin-vanillin scent of old books that I can read on the wicker futon by the window. A porcelain sink juts out of the wall near the bed. It feels out of place until you need a palm full of water in the middle of the night.

There's an empty wine bottle and three beer cans piled into a clear acrylic plastic box on the ground. A foolproof system I've developed for protecting floors and drinks. If something spills, it spills in the box. When I'm being disgusting and desperate I can tilt the box into my mouth. Last night it accumulated a wine-beer mixture, bitter tannins floating in carbonated hops that dry my tongue out.

I get up at noon and take my coffee on the front porch, looking across the street to Megan's house. Another Jorgenson & Jorgenson heiress. J&J is actually a bunch of Smiths and Wilsons and Grants in a trench coat. I'm a Grant, she's a Wilson. Our grandparents bought Victorian beach houses on the same block so they could spend their summers together. Or keep an eye on each other. One summer her grandpa started to cut newspaper into strips and build little boxes. I saw him cross the street to the hotel, presenting a tiny paper cube with six versions of Colin Powell's face to a confused tourist in cutoffs. A few years later, a financial advisor convinced him to sell most of his assets, including the Victorian mansion.

I don't eat until sundown to get my money's worth off the bar's beach town prices. After four beers I turn my book upside down for attention. It works. I don't want to get into his car or show him where I live, but I know a spot.

Brett's parents' house was built in the 90s and has a clean, spacious kitchen, stocked with every cooking gadget, sauce, and spice under the sun. The spices have been in direct sunlight for years and get a little musty, but taste fine. Especially when I lean over and deglaze the pan with a splash of my Grenache. He's impressed. His hairline is receding and his biceps are bigger than his head and his rimless glasses mean he doesn't get much. He doesn't understand how. His ugly glasses make me feel like a candle in a dessert. A torched brûlée. He's going to say and do and feel anything the moment calls for. He's already living in the future where he's telling the story of tonight. Before I serve him dinner he runs his hand under the string of Brett's mom's apron. I kick him out around 2 AM and sleep in Brett's room alone.

It got cold overnight. I go through his closet for a jacket that'll look good on me. Perfectly oversized. He has hunting fatigues and neon orange beanies and waders and fishing poles and woah that's a long gun. I carry it downstairs under my arm and lay it on the couch for a moment. There are boogie boards and beach towels and umbrellas in the basement. I take one of the umbrellas apart and go upstairs with the case. Striped white and red Tommy Bahama. It fits the gun perfectly. I put the key back in the lockbox and bike half an hour home with the gun slung across my chest, weighing me down at turns. The shore was silent as a beach of seagull feathers, a Jimenez poem. 60 degrees and foggy. Morning dew, silence, and stray cats. The only time I've seen cats around here is at dawn, when they run back and forth, dunes to dumpsters. They never take the boardwalk. The foggy salt air makes me think about how I've never tried an oyster. It's a risk. Someone could see me grimace, hate it, not understand it, let it win. I'd be relegated to the circle of hell with people who peel grapes and wash chicken. I could try one alone in my bedroom where no one could see, but what would be the point? An oyster is a celebration: champagne, caviar, fireworks, and four inch heels.

I sleep for six more hours until I put on a silk scarf and red lipstick and bike to the fish market. I call on one of the Serbian fishmongers behind the counter and ask for a batch of fresh oysters. I kick myself for the signifier when I see the Serb smirk. Now he's going to dig to the bottom of the bushel and give me the oldest, ripest, sickest oysters. He's going to trick me, give me a handful of clams at the bottom of my bag. The ones you see licking their chops on TV, old and fat and swelling out of their shells.

I stop at Acme and buy Castelvetrano olives, pearled couscous, and a lemon. Then Collier's for white wine and a case of Narragansett. The beer is heavy so I walk my bike the two blocks home.

A second batch of kids and parents are milling around Megan's porch and the street. Some kind of career-focused summer camp, I guess. Kids who get good grades and have never gotten their asses kicked by anyone but their parents. Their brows knit up as I pass by with my oysters and beer.

I spread out on the porch and crack open a Narragansett. I get a little high and it makes me pensive and anxious and I intricate myself into the neuroses of everyone I'm spying on. I read the kids' and parents' faces like a TV special.
The cast of characters:

Tall hairy kid with a slight hunchback: Quick goodbye hugs with his dad. One suitcase.
Shirtless ginger kid: already rearing to go for a swim. He'll be so disappointed by the cold.
Short, chubby mixed girl: Suffocating white mom with gray curly hair and a silk scarf around her neck. Her black dad is tall and bald and friendly to everyone. They probably still have sex.
Maybe this is her chance to finally get some sleep.
Chaperone 1: Drew Barrymore's character in Donnie Darko. Add 15

years.

Chaperone 2: Super energetic Latino with a high and tight haircut and motor mouth. The only person helping everyone with their bags.

All the black and Mexican kids' parents are so proud of them. They're taking group photos in front of the house. Someone's frizzy mom already bought an I HEART CAPE MAY sweatshirt. Maybe she was just cold. It's overcast here until Memorial Day. Through Memorial Day, really, but the bodies make it warmer. The kinetic beehive of umbrellas on the beach. They're so cheap for renting this off season. The kids can't even swim.

I get bored of them all and go upstairs.

*

I sit in the widow's walk and watch Megan's house. The ginger kid is rubbing sunblock on his chest on the front porch. Back for more. Maybe the water isn't as bad as I thought. I throw on a bathing suit, put blush on my cheeks, and leave with a towel, novel, snacks, and beer.

The ginger's name is Sam. Or Sean. He's 17 and sufficiently impressed by a case of beer and a hand on his thigh. A forbidden nature preserve sends him over the edge. I lead him to slaughter in the Endangered Tern Nesting Area.

"Are you sure it's okay for the birds to be eating Cap'n Crunch?"

"They love it." I throw another handful to the seagulls and Endangered Terns. "Let's go find some ghost crabs once the sun goes down. It's fun to shine a flashlight and watch them scatter."

"I can't."

"Tomorrow morning?"

"The first day of the RLE conference is tomorrow. *Raytheon Leaders in Education.* Maybe you can come."

"You know where to find me."

The sun is setting behind Colliers and I buy a 6 pack connected by that plastic 888 that chokes turtles. I rip one off at a time on my walk towards the playground. I rip #3 off the plastic and drink it on the swing. When it feels empty enough I smash it on my forehead and drop it to the ground. I keep swinging. I drop my arms behind me, leaning back, thighs clinging to the rubber seat, feet dragging against the ground. The momentum of the swing's chains swing me back and forth, my hair and arms dragging upside down against wood chips. It feels like the ocean.

It occurs to me in a shock of joy that the ocean is less than a mile away. I'm so happy to be drunk and walking alone by myself at night. I can't think of anywhere else I could do this but supersterile Victorian Cape May. There's a big helicopter that beams infrared and scoops up vagrants, bums, criminals, and undesirables into a crab net and releases them over the Delaware Bay, Pinochet-style.

Not really.

The local public servants give every homeless person they see a $200 hotel voucher and a bus ticket to Atlantic City.

I check on the ghost crabs that live in the cracks between the big wet rocks of the jetty. They scatter as soon as I appear. They've seen the Old Bay banner plane flying over crab eaters opening beers with their Old Bay keychains on their Old Bay beach towels. I see one pinch my foot, coming for his reparations. I let him have it. My reflexes are gone and I'm too drunk to feel his pincer. If he wants a toe, he can take a toe, I've got nine more lives.

I leave my clothes in the lifeguard roost and go for a swim. I sink my chin down into the water when the beach cleaner drives by in his big noisy truck. The ocean is cold and winds me and I could drown but I'm not so lucky.

*

I take my coffee on the front porch. I tense up when Sean waves towards me. He walks over and reminds me about the RLE conference.
"It's in the convention center on the boardwalk."
  "A block away from the arcade. I know it."
  "Are you coming?"
  "Am I allowed?"
  "Not quite."
  "I'll go."

Sean gives me another girl's lanyard. She has IBS and wants to stay home and watch cable. The barcode works and I'm in. Every tenth person in here is probably clocking me for a fake high schooler like they're watching a Lifetime movie. Maybe it's just hangover anxiety. My lanyard's strap is decorated with the logos of NASA, NOAA, Samsung, McGraw Hill, Treyarch, and Anheuser-Busch. I want to show someone my ID and get an orange wristband but can't blow my cover. We walk around the convention center collecting lanyards, pens, drawstring backpacks, and koozies. We take fistfuls of candy while a chubby DOD contractor pitches an internship building satellites in Baltimore. We try astronaut food from a tube and spit it out into SpaceX napkins. I follow Sean into a room full of computer screens and gaming consoles. The walls are lined with thin bands of neon light, like laser tag. A girl scans our lanyards as we come in. She's wearing more makeup than me and looks good in khakis and I want to leave.

"Two to a system."

We sit down and I wipe the fingerprints off my controller before pressing start.

The game has four levels, each in a different location:

Practice: Antarctica. Sporadic targets running across an open white plain.

Beginner: Middle Eastern or Saharan desert. Targets popping out from a row of bases. Intermittent sandstorms blinding the shooter. I looked around and saw that most kids were getting weeded out by the landmines. Sean figured out that you can quickly win this round if you change over to night mode and power up to some green goggles. The Desert Storm strategy.

Intermediate: A heavily wooded warzone on a mountain. Enemy combatants growling in something Eastern European, sneaking through the forest. Their grenades launch avalanches that'll kill you if you don't run up the mountain fast enough.

Expert: A busy city with a mix of modern architecture and old limestone buildings that look like museums. A number of civilians walking around at a brisk European pace, weaving through streets and fountains and squares and cafes. One of the Expert level targets is a red ballerina. She's easy to find because she circles the square in a 3 minute loop like the rest of the NPCs. She walks down the marble steps of the grand pillared theater in a red leotard, pink tights, and white scrunchie. Shooting her gets you 700 points, but there's a catch; every time you shoot her, your power ups disable for 30 seconds. Your camouflage stops working, rendering you visible to all other snipers for 30 seconds without being able to fire back. The only way to win this round is to let her run around Rome/Paris/Milan/Moscow until the very end of the round.

I get bored of watching Sean beat every level twice and go get a wristband. When the bartender is putting on my paper corsage I notice the underside of my arm is pale as a fishbelly. I alternate drink stations until a teenager taps me on the shoulder and asks if I'd like to try out a VR headset.

"Would you like to be an astronaut, pilot, or submarine officer?

Astronauts are corny and the idea of a submarine makes me feel short of breath. "Pilot."

He straps me in, pulling my hair a few times, jostling my drink. "You'll watch a three minute loop of a pilot taking off and striking. Remember, you don't have a controller, it's only VR, so just relax and watch. Don't worry about pressing any buttons or making any moves."

The plane takes off and I start to get dizzy and grab onto the kid for balance. He's so skinny. Maybe I'm holding on to a folding chair with a sweatshirt thrown over it. The pilot strikes the center of a mountain and the bomb lands in a big wet slosh of magma that covers my windshield. I reach for the wipers. I touch someone's cold hands. I take the goggles off, trying not to think of what my hair looks like, or the inevitable pink line on my forehead.

"How was it?" he asks, wiping my headset off with rubbing alcohol. I feel a little offended that he's doing that in front of me. I get my fifth drink and leave to go watch the ocean from the veranda. It's the warmest day yet. I hop the fence, land in sand, and start taking my shorts off. I fold my clothes into a pillow and settle in for a tan. My last drink is starting to hit me and my purse spills onto the sand. I reach for my lipstick, that classic little MAC bullet that feels so good in my hand. I draw a red circle around my belly button as a plane flies above me. I shoot him with my finger a few times and fall asleep.

The beach is the only place where you can walk around with a bathing suit under your clothes all day, start drinking at 11, nap it off on the sand, and go about your evening.

At home I arrange the oysters in a circle on ice, squeeze lemon on their bellies, and tweeze the stray citrus seeds off the plate with chopsticks. I iron my hair like Veronica Lake and draw a beauty mark on my cheek like Marilyn. I dance around the kitchen until I catch my reflection. The beauty mark looks stupid and I smudge a brown line across my face wiping it off. It took 40 minutes to do my makeup. Liner from the inner corner to the outer, highlight on my cheek and brow bones, coral blush that would look clownish in daylight. Red lips, fake lashes, high contrast. Grandma's red silk bathrobe. Angelina * Monica * Helen of Troy. Drunk in a kitchen built in 1841. I thought of the panopticon, the boredom, the suffocation, a woman would feel in this room 100 years ago. I'll be throwing up into 200 year old pipes tomorrow morning and be freer than a woman dropping belladonna in her eye while a slave gives birth in the little house behind ours. The one we sold in the 80s. Some woman from Texas moved in and had a stroke while gardening 10 years later. I've never seen anyone go in there but the little backyard skunk.

My ice is melting and my olives are starting to sweat but I feel nice and drunk and go upstairs to the widow's walk to watch the kids across the street. They're having a party with strobe lights in their living room that illuminate their silhouettes identically. Brett's gun fits perfectly in the hole between the screen and the window frame. Just a thin little nose on such a long gun.

Sean walks outside onto the porch. More kids follow him and turn to face the house, leaning back against the Victorian gingerbread railing, pushing against its antique limits. A camera flash goes off and my trigger finger follows. The bullets sound distant, like they're coming from the ocean. I empty the gun into their gingerbread railing and watch kids fall onto the porch. Horizontal and parallel in matching sweatshirts.

A cop asks me questions an hour later. He sees my melted ice and submerged oysters and cried-off makeup and believes I've been stood up.

"It's never happened to me before. Maybe he heard the shooting and got spooked."

"You think he's a witness?"

Any name I give him, real or fake, could cause trouble.

"I met him the old fashioned way. On the boardwalk. Never got his name."

"Ma'am, did you notice your refrigerator is unplugged?"

The cop leaves without even checking upstairs. I think he felt the ghosts too. After he's gone I blow kisses to the ghosts and give them nicknames. Shelly, Hadrian, Marlon, and Pearl. I thank them all. I pour Malbec into four glasses and set them around the long dinner table in their honor. I crawl across the oriental carpet, Shelly's goblet in my hand, raised to the heavenly hosts of 36 Congress St. Too drunk to walk upstairs, I crawl into my tent and sleep in there for the night.

I take my coffee on the front porch. Five of the kids, including Sean, are wrapped up in blankets on Megan's wicker. I go back inside.

Flour, butter, sugar, salt.

There's rust on this pastry cutter and no one at the kitchen table. I imagine Hadrian sitting there, grumpy and hungover with an Irish coffee, watching me bake. I make a batch of sugar cookies with cinnamon-vanilla icing and carry the tray over to Megan's. I've done this before, when her aunt got married to a Libertarian.

I set the tray down on the coffee table. Sean says hi with his eyes.

Drew looks solemn and nods her head, charging herself up for a courteous remark about the cookies. I'm nervous under her silence and accidentally call her the nickname I've given her. She frowns, unfamiliar. I catch my reflection in the windowpane behind her head and for a moment I feel a painful clarity. Now *I'm* Mr. Wilson, the senile neighbor bearing unwanted gifts, only tolerated for my proximity and wealth. If she's Drew Barrymore in Donnie Darko, I'm Drew Barrymore in Grey Gardens. I cross the street back home and sleep for 12 hours.

Flags are at half mast but stores are open. The French bakery was bought out by Bulgarians a few years ago. They kept the name and the glass case of familiar pastries, but put in a refrigerator full of farmer's cheese, cured meats, and pierogies all labeled in Cyrillic. I bought a batch of walnut sticky buns and two croissants. I thought of the first time Graham joined me on this early morning breakfast mission. We held hands in the foggy morning, taking the shortcut behind the seafood restaurants, poking each other every time we saw an alley cat or Eastern European lifeguard on her walk of shame. They never took the boardwalk either.

They stopped importing lifeguards to the East Coast, it's all locals in the roosts again. I wonder what that means for the culture.

I fry an egg and put it between the two croissants. The ghosts' wine is giving the dining room an acidic smell. The house feels barren. I think I scared them away. The piece of folded cardboard stabilizing one leg of the dinner table is disintegrating into the oriental carpet. Paranoia is setting in. I change the combination on the lockbox to 6879, a year that hasn't happened and never will. I drive 40 minutes down Garden State Parkway and turn off when I see the perfect swamp. I throw Brett's gun into the reeds and watch it sink into methane-scented water, imagining it was a spoon falling into a cup of gritty black tea.

Heart of a Dog

I WAS BROWSING coats for my ski trip with the in-laws when I noticed Helen of Troy picking out knives at the REI. The blades were under glass, guarded by a wiry teenager wearing a wide paisley headband over his curly mess. She was a head taller than him, with dark hair, dark eyes, dark lips. He looked like he could curl up into a ball and fit into one of her muscular, equestrian thighs. She wore heeled snakeskin boots that went halfway up her calves, with laces that wound higher, a spiral staircase to heaven. She tapped an acrylic nail at a suede holster and asked if she could try it on. When she raised her arms slightly as he kneeled in front of her to fasten it, her tight fur-trimmed parka rode up to reveal a dangling diamond belly piercing. Her long hair ended at the waistband of her low rise jeans. The teen's knuckles grazed her skin as he tied the sling around her hips, sucking in his bottom lip. He'd cut his ear off for her. I could watch her pick out knives forever.

I hovered close to the checkout, scrutinizing carabiners, dictaphone in my pocket, thumb over the red rubber button, hoping she'd say *yes, I do have a phone number with REI*. She hardly opened her mouth when she talked to the cashier; her words crawled out the side of her lips like a trickle of ants. Her voice was deep, accented, reluctantly feminine. I couldn't make out a single word.

She got into the backseat of a black SUV waiting for her in the parking lot. The man driving caught my eye. I pretended to take a call and tried to stay three cars behind them. Three could have been overkill, who remembers a dark green Camry?

They parked in a strip mall and she went into Nina's Nails. I got a little paranoid and drove back to work at the animal control office.

14

I thought about how my wife said she was tired of going to Asian nail salons; she couldn't understand them or read their faces and it made for some Sisyphean small talk. Shira would come home with a beautiful set of red nails and a depressed mood.

"But this one had great reviews, what happened?"

"They make them wear fake name tags that read 'Jane' and 'Grace'. It's abject."

That weekend I tricked Shira into thinking we were running errands and drove her to Nina's Nails. She wrapped her little hands around my face and kissed my earlobe, *thank you thank you I love surprises*. I felt warm and useful and clever from a place below my ribs.

The moment the door chimed behind us I saw Shira's face fall a little, realizing this nail salon was the *other* kind of Caucasian. A tiny brunette in a ripstop tracksuit and dirty sneakers was curled up on a couch near the window, resting her head on a large backpack, engrossed in *Teen Vogue*. A heavily perfumed and made up woman greeted us from the front desk. Her breasts were as big as her head, a little bigger than Shira's. She spoke polite broken English with a nasally snarl. She seemed like the madame of the nail salon—her bossiness was undercut with practiced diplomacy. The madame directed Shira to a puffy leather chair in the back of the salon and asked her to pick her polish.

"Dina!" The madame barked at Tracksuit. *"Osvobodi mesto pendosam."*

Tracksuit jumped up and offered me her loveseat. She sat on her haunches nearby and placed the magazine on the floor in front of her. *Clear a space for the 'pendos,'* I jotted down in my notebook, where my thoughts wait before I record them in the privacy of my car. My useless Russian literature degree from IU would keep me entertained today.

The madame took Shira's puffer off for her, gently, one sleeve at a time. I made a note to do the same once we got home, make her feel pampered. A tall girl with a flat, Kazakh face brought a bundle of my wife's coat and purse back to me. She and my wife were the only smiling women in the room. I wondered if I was wrong to interpret the Kazakh's high cheekbones and narrow almond eyes as warmth when they were probably just frozen into an ambiguous Steppe expression. A sturdy blonde girl in gold earrings and a plunging blue top took a washcloth out of a towel warmer and put it around Shira's neck. She introduced herself as Sasha and asked her how the water felt. She spoke perfect English, and I knew Shira wouldn't mind her saccharine affectation. I relaxed into the couch.

Tracksuit was filling out a personality quiz using little dots of blue nail polish in lieu of a pen. I offered her mine, but she shook her head no thank you, this way she could erase her scores afterwards, with a Q-tip and a little acetone. I was quietly grateful that she turned me down, this way I could continue writing down the Russian words and phrases being flung around the salon. I wasn't sure what possessed me to offer it up, other than the girl's sweet expression in her downturned brown eyes, or the way she chewed on her cuticles and rocked back and forth in childlike focus. I wanted to give her a dish of cream.

The door chimed, announcing the arrival of two identical men who caught the gaze of every woman in the salon, even Shira. They were tall and buzzed, a centimeter of dark hair sheared over two brutalist skulls and angular jaws. Their faces were the color of cement after rain.

"Are they twins?" I whispered to Tracksuit.
    "Yeah. Lazar and Zakhar." She was counting up her score on her fingers, starting over after answering my question.
    "Cool. Sorry for messing you up."
    "It's okay. I'm slow at counting."
    "Are they her sons?"
    She laughed and shook her head. She kept looking over at the madame, who was kissing the twins' foreheads and running her nails over their cropped scalps. I could tell my line of questioning was making her nervous, and let her be. I pulled out my notebook and kept writing down words as I heard them. *Platezhka. Sobaki. Anya. Toyota Highlander.* Something about dogs and money. The twin carrying a rolled up canvas bag went into the little room where women get Brazilian waxes. I saw Shira smile at him when he walked past her, nodding at her and all of the other ladies getting pedicures. Asshole. I went outside for a smoke.

A black SUV was running in the parking lot. New York plates, yellow like a taxi. 4733 LKM. I jotted it down. The woman from REI was sitting in the middle of the backseat, leaning forward to adjust the heat.

I panicked and went back inside and paid for Shira's manicure. Tracksuit came out of the bathroom with damp hair, like she'd just washed it in the sink. The madame gave her a scowl that immediately snapped back to a close-lipped smile when she caught my glance. "Come back again with your lovely wife!"

I couldn't sleep that night. I ran my fingertips over Shira's fresh lacquer, slippery against my skin. I wish she was awake to scratch my back. I kept thinking about the Russians; knife girl, the twins, the madame, and the homeless girl in the tracksuit. I went downstairs with my notebook and pulled up an online translator.

*

"You have to keep me anonymous. I *mean* it." Dina picked grains of cilantro-lime rice off her tracksuit. Her mood shifted as soon as she was satiated. I'd never seen anyone eat so quickly.

I'd driven in circles around the strip mall where I'd first met her at the salon. I had two beef burritos in my cooler. I ate one in front of a Korean restaurant an hour before I saw her on the shoulder near 7/11, covering roadkill with pine branches and discarded newspaper.

She started shifting her feet over the trash in my passenger seat. Her anxiety was becoming contagious. I handed her another $20.

"I don't know your last name, anyways."
   "It bothers me that you even know my first."
   "How about I give you a codename, something simple. Lara?"
   "Like Dr. Zhivago? They made us read that in school. I hated it."
   I love that movie. I pressed her about the twins again.
   "Lazar, Zakhar, and their sister, Agrippa, have a deal with some illegal puppy mills around here. They threaten to shut them down unless they pay up once a month. Anywhere from 1-3 grand a month. Then they run that money through Inna's salon, and she keeps a little for herself."
   "How do they find the puppy mills?"
   "That part's easy. People talk. They can't shut up about their cute new Samoyed or Shiba or Chihuahua. They brag to everyone at the salon, church, Facebook…word travels. The sneaky ones? Agrippa finds them

through work, real estate. Someone calls to rent a pet-friendly place with an enclosed backyard, claiming they have four emotional support dogs. She rents it to them, and then her brothers visit a month later. That kind of thing."

"Are they dangerous?"

"No, people just hand over all that money because they're so *charming*." She rolled her eyes.

We sat in silence for a few beats.

"I'm sorry, thank you for the food." She folded her arms across her chest and tucked her head down. "I shouldn't have said anything. I don't want any trouble with the Hlavacs, or Inna. But I hate puppy mills. I wish you'd shut them all down. And my stomach hurts, I don't usually eat meat."

"I didn't know you were a vegetarian."

She shrugged. "Eating animals is disgusting. Have you ever seen meat hanging off wire hangers and shopping carts around parking lots, or in alleyways? That's the shit you're eating. There's a place a block away that does that, a few feet away from their dumpsters. I can show you. You'd swear off meat for life."

"So you're not a bleeding heart animal lover?" I teased. "Just a germaphobe?"

"I'll show you right now!" She got up in her seat. "Right behind East Pearl. Some kinda rat-looking things hanging off of coat hangers by a pile of trash. If that makes me a germaphobe..."

I knew the spot. I took Shira there for our eighth wedding anniversary last month.

"I'll bring you pizza next time. Maybe you'll pace yourself better that way."

"I was hungry."

"Maybe they're just dog people?"

"They're extortionists, not vigilantes. The only thing Agrippa hates more than dogs is people who create more of them."

I stepped out to take a call. I pulled the phone away from my mouth so the woman on the other end couldn't hear my teeth chatter. I watched Dina warm her hands on my vents, alternating the fronts and backs.

"Want to come along?" I handed her one of my Montgomery County Animal Control windbreakers from the backseat. She zipped it up over her tracksuit, nylon swishing against nylon.

We pulled into the driveway of a corner lot, right by the mouth of a hiking trail.

"This woman saw a raccoon climb down her tree and evacuated to a hotel for the night."

"Nice porch." Dina ran over to a wooden deck chair and started to rock in it. She settled back with her arms on the throne and surveyed the yard like a patriarch. "So we just sit here and wait for a coon to show up? Don't we need a cage or something?"

"Unless I see something frothing at the mouth, I'm not doing shit. We get calls like these all the time. People think that if they see a raccoon in the daylight, it must be rabid. But they aren't nocturnal, they're crepuscular. They lay low to avoid humans."

We collected leaves and sticks for the fire pit in an orange Home Depot bucket.

"What are you going to do with the Hlavacs?" She asked, warming her hands against the fire.

"Why does their name sound like a hairball?"

Dina laughed and tucked her dirty sneakers underneath herself, Indian style. "Because they're Serbian-Czech-Russian mutts." Her eyes, nose and cheeks were pink, and her cheekbone had a little speck of glitter, some vagabond eyeshadow that had traveled south. "What are you, Wyatt? An exotic blend of Anglo-Saxon? Don't tell me you're Irish."

"I'm gonna try to bust up some puppy mills. Follow them around a little, use their leads?"

She put her feet down on the grass and stopped smiling.

"You wanna hear what they did a few weeks ago?"

I coughed loudly as I hit the rubber side button on my dictaphone, hoping she didn't hear the click.

"There's this lady, Anya, who works at one of the Russian schools. You know, where immigrant families, or moms who married American dudes send their kids so they don't forget how to speak Russian?"

"Like those Chinese Saturday schools, yeah."

"Not really, there's no multiplication tables or SAT prep, just grammar, poems, art classes, and little holiday plays. Every Russian woman with a pulse has worked in one at some point. Anyway, Anya advertised her side business on the school's Facebook before Easter. She breeds rabbits and Borzois. *Think* about that for a moment. She's a sick fuck."

It seemed like an economical system; cold, but practical, self sufficient, a closed loop. I felt guilty for the thought and let Dina keep talking.

"Someone at the salon mentioned it to Inna, who told Agrippa, who told Anya that she had two months to come up with three grand or she'd set her rabbit coop on fire. Anya told her to fuck off. There was a little back and forth for a few months, and then in September, when school started back up, things started to escalate."

I shifted in my seat, angling my hip towards Dina to make sure my dictaphone was picking up her voice.

"One morning, as class was starting, suddenly all these kids are fucking screaming and crying in Anya's classroom. They opened up their pencil cases to find a little bloody rabbit ear in every single one."

"Jesus. Did Anya pay up?"

"No. And I heard she started breeding snakes, too."

*

I thought about Dina's story after I dropped her off at the bus station. I wondered if I was stupid enough to risk it. It would be nice to finally have something to talk about with Shira and the in-laws on vacation. The address Dina gave me wasn't too far from work. I could park near the Hlavacs' townhouse, see where they drive to, get a couple leads on illegal breeders. No harm in jotting down some addresses to show Terry at work and see what happens.

Six years of driving around, passing by rundown houses with high fences, driveways full of bricks and tarps, windows obscured with cardboard or tapestries; imagining how it would feel to kick down front doors and come back out with armfuls of fleabitten Golden puppies, come out a hero. But instead my days are trapping raccoons and euthanizing foxes and muzzling dogs. Terry said not to bother with puppy mills, it's a good way to get stabbed and fed to a pack of Rottweilers. Every weekend the Salvadorians host dogfights behind Clock Tower Liquor in Aspen Hill, right in the parking lot. But *we don't carry guns,* Terry reminds me.

I sat in the driveway, watching my wife watch TV with the dogs. I clicked record on my dictaphone:

> "The perfect woman is a chimera of a cat and a deer, or maybe a cat and a horse, standing on herbivorously large haunches and polished hooves. Her face is bright and flushed, round cheeks over a delicate chin, heart shaped and feline. Her hair is thick as a girl's, but long as time, long as an old mare's, a relic of the human penchant for holding on and never letting go. The past is the feathers with which we stuff our beds, we pad the present with what cannot be changed. The future is an afterthought. We plow through living forests to build retro diners, where the jukebox is full of tired songs and rusty coins…
>
> I've been fantasizing about a high priestess, with beauty that screams through her modest neckline, revealing nothing but collarbone. Her nose is long and pointed, foxlike. Her hair is long and dark and thick as a cloak. She's wearing an embroidered coat sewn from elk leather, with mink trim, and an embroidered headdress laden with coins, riding on the back of a Przewalski…"

My neighbor's headlamp grew closer to my window.

Click.

"Wyatt! Did you see my note this morning?" Connie flat-palm banged on my window in her headlamp and Yale sweatshirt. I got out of the car and hoped she wouldn't shine her headlamp towards the recycling bin, where her pink Post-it note was crumpled up on top of beer cans and milk jugs.

"I didn't, busy week. Busting up a dog breeding network in Rockville. *Russian* puppy mills."

"I need you to take a look at this illegal drainage pipe the Sterns installed last week. They're pouring chemicals into my pond and killing my fish."

"Connie, I don't do fish."

"Of course you do fish. If you don't do fish, no one does fish. Who am I supposed to turn to? Do you know how much a single koi costs, Wyatt?"

"We don't. I don't. I don't know what else to tell you. But I'll come take a look, *as a neighbor*, tomorrow morning."

"8 AM. And wear your uniform."

My uniform was a polyester polo shirt with Montgomery County Animal Control shyly embroidered over my heart. I appreciated Connie's faith in my authority. I went back inside and kissed my wife and dogs on the heads.

"I made another appointment for that Russian salon tomorrow. Could you take me at lunch?"

Shira's breath smelled like cinnamon and paprika and I knew she'd been eating my Skyline Chili.

*

I waited in the car this time, recording, hoping I'd see Agrippa in the parking lot again.

> "I overheard a girl talking about Nabokov at the bar last night… I wanted to interject, but she could have been on a date. If it was a date, he was really punching up. Southern, bald fellow. A little out of shape. She said *Invitation to a Beheading* was the only quality work he had ever produced; *Lolita* and *Ada* were lascivious money grabs, his chess novels were boring, and *Gift* should have been renamed *Grift*… a cheap ride on Dostoevsky and Chernyshevky's coattails. She said "Vova" spat on his aristocratic upbringing to reject Christ, to hide behind his faith, his Vera, his Jewish wife…just to come to the US so he

could lecture at Cornell in cargo shorts. That's when her date went to the bathroom, and I saw that he was wearing cargo shorts over his long johns…"

Dina jumped into my passenger seat.
  Click.
  "What's that, you recording your memoirs?"
  "Just my thoughts and observations."
  "Listen, shit's going down at Anya's on Friday. Pick me up in the morning, I can find her address by then." She handed me her number scribbled on a 7/11 receipt.

*

Dina got into my car a couple blocks away from the strip mall.
  "Do you know anywhere I could get a gun?"
  "Yeah." She directed me down Nichols Lane to the Petco. I wondered if it was weird to wear my Animal Control fatigues in a pet store and grabbed my shearling jacket instead of the windbreaker.

She ran up to a skinny blonde who was carrying a dog crate under his arm, pale blue eyes ringed with mauve dark circles. He could have been in his late teens or late twenties, that ambiguous way Slavs look like teenagers pushing middle age.

"Pavel, Wyatt."

He put his free arm around her skinny neck and whispered something I couldn't make out for the most part, and some words I'd heard at the salon. *Pendos.* Pouring ants into her ear. Ants holding up little scraps of newspaper, each holding a letter spelling out *fuck you Wyatt*.

"He said he can help you. Go wait for him over there, where they groom dogs."
  "Are you coming?"
  "I'll be with the fish, doing Pasha's job for him."
  I didn't last five minutes inside the glass box, waiting next to a trembling shih-tzu. I followed her to the aquarium section.

Her windbreaker was on a chair, sleeves rolled up, elbow deep in a tank full of aquarium plants. Sludgy kelps and torn leaves and green gravel. She was trying to catch something with a little green net.

"Pasha is an asshole. Everyone who works here is a psychopath." She wiped a splash of dirty water off her cheek. "There are three Siamese Fighting Fish in the plant tank, and they're all trying to kill each other. They fight, they get exhausted, they pass out on an Amazon Sword Plant, they get a glimpse of each other through the Hornwort, and then the cycle begins again. I don't even think they feed them in here. They just fight, sleep, and eat dead snails."

"Do you want me to say something to him?"
    "Knock yourself out."
    "I changed my mind about the gun."
    She dropped the net and glared at me.
    "Sorry. I didn't think I said that so loudly. Can we get out of here?"
    "Once I separate them."

An indigo fish with a red-tinged tail was undulating against the glass in the bottom corner, trapped by a mess of plants that looked like submerged dill. I showed Dina and she rushed over with her net, her windbreaker pants swishing next to my jeans. She moved him to another section of the tank, separated by a panel of glass covered in hairy blue-green algae. The section of plants she moved him to already had a white and purple fish, barely breathing, at the bottom of the tank. I didn't have the heart to point it out to her and left to check out the other fish tanks.

Clownfish, angelfish, the blue thing from *Finding Nemo*; the saltwater fish had some kind of exotic dignity above the tanks full of belly-up goldfish and pregnant guppies. A Moray eel stalked a dirty tank by itself, banished to solitary confinement for its meanness, its ugliness. One tank was labeled glass catfish, $7.99. Completely transparent slivers of flesh, tiny knives of glass with white whiskers and little black hearts beating for everyone to see. I couldn't bear it. I balled up Dina's windbreaker and led her out of the Petco by her wet little arm.

*

"I think we're here. This is the address she gave 'Lara', the prospective Borzoi buyer."

"I'll park around the corner."

Dina put her hair in a high ponytail, flipped it across the top of her head so the ends hung over her forehead, and tucked them under a headband to make it look like she had bangs. She put the Animal Control beanie over this contraption of hair, and arranged it to look like she was a teenage boy with flow.

"Can't be recognized."

"You got a purty mouth, Dennis."

"Gimme a toothpick."

"Take my sunglasses. Just lay low."

We waited for half an hour until the black SUV pulled up in front of Anya's. A small blonde with rodentlike features and thin blonde hair, dark at the roots, came out of the front door. She whistled twice and a white pitbull latched into Lazar's upper arm. Zakhar grabbed the dog's hind legs and Agrippa stabbed it twice in the neck. She wiped the blade on its fur before putting it back into her holster. Anya threw two metal lawn chairs at Agrippa, missing her twice by a hair.

"Tsiganka! Ved'ma bezdushnaya!"

Dina saw me write it down. "She called her a gypsy and a soulless witch. Do you think she killed it?"

The dog jumped back up and started chasing Agrippa to the SUV, her brothers shielding themselves with lawn chairs as they backed towards the street. I started the car.

I looked over at Dina, hungry and cold. She didn't rescue any fish or dogs or rabbits today and was going to have to survive another night by herself in the dark. I turned my heat up high and put my jacket on top of her before I got out at the gas station. My chest ached after I dropped her off in the dark.

I played back my recordings in the driveway before I went inside my house.

"Hey. I'm sorry I went through your stuff, you're taking forever in the gas station, I wanted to smoke, and I found this thing... I heard the recording of us in the backyard, the story about Anya, and I deleted it. I got paranoid. There's this type of person who doesn't want to work, they *so desperately* don't want to work, so instead they just churn out animals or accumulate foster kids because it's so easy and there's nothing you can do about it, they'll do anything to keep— I see you coming out of the gas station, bye Wyatt, I hope you're not mad at me when you hear this..."

Click.

I passed by Anya's on the way to REI the next morning. The white dog was barking in her front yard, a shaved patch on its chest. A Salvadorian family next door was putting up a nativity display of Jesus, Mary, and two light up deer.

Dina was right. Animal control, social workers, we only exist to shuffle them around, look busy, have a number for Connies to call. All you can do is feed them, help them survive the winter, and pray they don't become roadkill. I spent my entire Christmas bonus at the REI: A coat for myself, cashmere gloves for my wife's beautiful little hands, and a set of thermals for Dina to wear under her tracksuit.

Entrails Over the Country Club

Vük HEARD his boss yelling over his shoulder as he folded his last stack of napkins into little fanfares in the center of the bridal party's dinner plates. He turned around on the third call, snapping up as he smelled his boss approaching. Sometimes he forgot his new name. He'd seen *Vük* glowing on a storefront two years ago, the neon sign for an arcade that sold pizza, beer, and skateboards. It was disorienting and comforting to see his native tongue in downtown Bethesda. He took it as a sign. Vük, meaning wolf, was a name Serbs gave their sons as a protective spell. The name on his burgundy passport was the name of an archangel but that bundle of paper was long gone, a handful of ashes somewhere in the Delaware River.

J&A J&A J&A sparkled in silver lettering all over the ballroom, all over the placemarkers and napkins and vases and pens tipped with square plastic cut to look like a big diamond. Fresh bouquets of lavender, heather, and forget-me-nots dripped petals onto white tablecloths. The Alaskan state flowers were a sentimental nod to when bride met groom on a chilly Northwestern cruise. Ever since that trip, Adeline fantasized about a winter wedding. Each place setting had a small gift bag with a jar of Lehua honey from Hawaii, a National Park Annual Pass, and a polaroid of the newlyweds.

Each drink station had a poster of the couple's signature cocktails. His was a rye Manhattan garnished with bergamot. Hers was an eye-catching blue mixture of elderflower liqueur and sparkling butterfly pea tea. The bartenders were trained to pour it in such a way that the cobalt *Clitoria* tea would rest at the bottom, creating an ombre effect. Adeline wanted balloon arches and pyramids of champagne, "like in *Babe 2*." Jonah wanted whatever Adeline wanted.

Vük daydreamed as he held a tray full of champagne flutes stuffed with sauced napkins and shrimp tails. He stood dead still except for his jaw that shifted side to side when he licked his teeth. The wealth on display that night was impressive. World Bank - Booz Allen money. Vük considered stealing a gift bag. Working weddings was a good time to eavesdrop. A good time to watch female relatives act out. What would happen to these women if they were completely deprived of attention for a day, a week, a month? Would they survive?

The maid of honor stood up to give a toast. Her mother nudged her in the thigh, handing her a cloth napkin. She shooed it away and wiped a blue beard of cupcake icing off her chin with her gauze shawl that strategically concealed the flushes of armpit swelling from her dress. Cherry, a brick-shit blonde in a pale blue bridesmaid's dress, layers upon layers of thin rayon that could be tied in six different ways. She tied hers behind her neck in a halter that pushed her breasts together so perfectly, her mother made her wear six strings of pearls to hide them. She didn't wear any underwear under her dress; she knew how many eyes would be on her ass while she bent down to fix her sister's train.

Cherry stopped mid-speech to pick a maraschino stem out of her molar. She dropped the nuisance on her plate, wiped her fingers against the tablecloth, and picked the microphone back up.

"They're cute," she slurred. "Real-fucking-cute. You could hand Jonah a jar of my sister's piss and he'd ask for a straw." Another bridesmaid took the microphone while the mother of the bride dragged Cherry away from the table. Father of the bride patted Adeline on the shoulder and excused himself to the seafood buffet.

The labyrinthian bathrooms opened with spacious lounges that fed into a room of stalls with doors that touched the ground. The groomsmen collected in the men's room further from the ballroom, smoking with their shoes muddying the damask futon under the bay window. Vük winced at the dirt on the silk brocade. The other week he had measured the window, measured the futon, and snapped his tape measure shut in disappointment that the wicker was much too wide to fit through the windowframe.

*

Cherry woke up cold and wet under a harsh white winter sky. A tall, skinny man was watching her, squatting on his haunches a few feet away. His straight dark hair fell over a narrow face; wind-warped forehead, deep set eyes, long teeth.

"It's perfectly safe up here. I've slept here a few times, when I was between places. I never got caught. It's a fairly new building. No HVAC issues, no leaks, nothing to fix yet."

He stood up and took a folded tarp off the pile he'd been sitting on.

"You understand what I'm getting at, right? No one is coming up here, not for months. Not unless the heater breaks. You stay under this during the day so the choppers don't see you. Not that there will be any. Some influential residents of Potomac Forest, namely, your parents and the rest of the HOA, banned them from hovering over their neighborhood. A little no-fly zone, if you will. They did it cleverly, too, invoking some kind of law protecting an endangered bird species, the Cerulean War-bler. Ever seen one of those? They're pretty. Bright blue like your dress."

He pulled something wrapped in a cloth napkin out of his backpack. She grabbed it hungrily, hoping it was something to eat. A small dead bird fell out onto her lap.

"I shot him this morning. You shouldn't throw him off your lap like that, he'll keep you company. I thought your family loved animals?"

Cherry started to cry and wrapped the bird back up into the napkin.

"You know, they are right about one thing. The birds are in danger, they're dying at a higher rate lately. I kept seeing dead fledgelings on the sidewalks this summer. I think it's something about the air, the fumes. Do you know anything about that? What they're *really* spraying out of those planes?"

Cherry shook her head, afraid to speak. She was on a roof, restrained, freezing, wearing nothing but her bridesmaid's dress and the stupid little shawl it came with.

"No laws against these, though." He pulled a small drone out his backpack. "35 hour battery life. I can make sure you've been a good girl, staying under the tarp during the day."

"There are people looking for me. My mom, my friends, Adeline, they're tearing everything apart searching for me. My family gives the cops a quarter of a million every five years."

Her desperation reminded him of the guppy darting around its tank, trying to avoid his encroaching stream of six sprays of Windex.

"Adeline's on her honeymoon."

"If you let me go now, I'll make something up, I'll tell them you rescued me. You won't get in trouble. My parents will probably even give you money."

"Let's talk about your parents for a moment. Ben and Cynthia, right?"

"Were they here? Did they come back here to look for me?"

"They did. The cops questioned everyone working that night, and we were very cooperative. We assured them that you got into a car around 10:30 the night of the wedding. There's even footage of it. Would you like to see?"

Cherry started to cry. "Did you show them? Does Adeline know?"

"Jonah's not in the video, somehow. You can't tell who was driving what from that angle, too much foliage. All you can see in that video is your blue dress getting into a black car."

"Are you one of Adeline's friends or something, punishing me?"

"I'll bring you meals at sunrise. You cool with leftovers?"

*

He threw a clear trash bag full of bread rolls and pats of butter wrapped in foil.

"This should keep you busy for a day or two. You don't look like a girl who's afraid of carbs."

He unpeeled a square of butter and spread it over his roll with a plastic knife. "You know your sister made us throw all this butter out? She

couldn't have *gold* butter wrappers at her *silver* wedding."
He saw Cherry eye the knife and threw it over his shoulder, out of her reach. She fanged a roll and then immediately started on another one, biting back and forth. Her blue fingers unpeeled three more pats of butter that she swallowed whole.

"Thank you. Thank you so much, Vuck."
   "Vük. Say it right."
   "*Vük*, Okay. Thank you. Where is that from?"

Her proclivity towards civility, her polite but insincere displays of interest, even in this scenario, amused him.

"It's Serbian."
   "Have you lived here long?"
   "A few years."
   "How many days have I been up here?" She'd tried to tally the days, carving them onto the frosted aluminum. He rubbed it off with his glove every morning.

He bent down and ripped off a layer of blue fabric from her dress. "You have ten minutes to bleed onto this. I need it covered. If you don't, I'll do it myself." He pulled out a serrated kitchen knife wrapped in a white napkin. Cherry started to bite the skin around her nails. Then she remembered all the times she'd cut her legs shaving, how much blood she had to wash off her tiles. She used the corner of her handcuffs to scrape a layer of skin off of her ankle and held it to the fabric.

"Did you plan this?" she asked, waiting for blue to turn red.
   "Did Jonah leave semen inside of you?"
   "I don't know."
   "Wipe."

Vük had seen Jonah carry Cherry out of his car and make her throw up in some bushes behind the kitchen. The groom was thirty minutes late to cut his own cake. It never made any sense to him, why American weddings cut the cake so late, when everyone's too drunk to hold a fork. Jonah left her curled up on the mulch. Vük woke her up and told her she was late for champagne on the roof. She was drunk to the point of canine obedience, silently climbing up the aluminum ladder all the way to the top. She looked confused for a moment; not scared, not panicked, but waiting for directions. She almost looked relieved when he tied her to a pipe with balloon string before going back to work.

*

Vük didn't really think she'd hold on this long on the roof without a coat in January. It had consistently dropped into the low 30s at night. Cherry was a sturdy girl. A good little waist, but thick in the arms and legs.

"Let me go, let my parents give you money. You won't have to work here anymore."

He watched her with a scalding silence.

"Is this about something I did? Or is this just about money? Are you waiting for them to pay a ransom?"

"The cops found part of your dress in the woods, covered in blood. I don't think they're in a generous mood."

"Is this about something *they* did?"

"Show me how smart you are, Cherry. Figure it out. Maybe you'll even get a prize."

"You knew my parents' names."

"They paid for the venue, of course I do."

"Do you know where they work?"

Cherry looked at the bulge of food in his plastic bag. She had been too cold to sleep the night before. She forgot what she wanted to say to him, something she planned last night, shivering under the stars.

"What did I do, Vük?"

He threw a ring of keys at her. "One of those opens up the handcuffs, four will let you into the HVAC units, and the rest are just janitor closets downstairs. I recommend the heating unit for this time of year." He presented his hands around a phantom bottle of wine.

Cherry tucked the keys under her thigh, afraid he'd change his mind. She waited for him to leave before taking them out. The key to the handcuffs was smaller than the rest. After she freed herself, she walked over to the door she saw him leave through and tried every key on the ring. Her hands were trembling and she kept starting over, losing her place in the keys. Her fingers were too numb to take the ones she'd already tried off the ring. She licked condensation off the aluminum walls until she could piss on her hands to warm them up. Her feet were so numb she could barely walk, so she tried crawling to the six-foot safety fence that lined the perimeter of the roof fifteen feet away from the edge. She took off one of her necklaces and threw it, clearing the fence but not the roof. Her mother's pearls clattered on the wet concrete a few feet away from her. The sun was setting and she tried one last time to find the right key. She wrapped balloon string around the ones she'd tried. He'd taken off the key to the exit. The sun was setting. She gave up and tried the HVAC units. She felt their walls to see which one was the heater, but they all felt cold to the touch. One of the keys wrapped in blue balloon string fit perfectly. She turned the key and swung the door open. The unit smelled mildewy, revolting, like a dirty pond, but she wanted to sleep out of the wind. Two tarps like the one she'd been sleeping under were rolled up in the back behind the A/C. She pulled one out to unroll it but it was heavier than she thought and slipped out of her numb fingers. She pulled it from the bottom and the smell grew. She unrolled two tarps before she saw two blue-gray feet in strappy sandals sticking out.

She locked the door behind her and handcuffed herself back to the pole.

"You didn't find the key?" Vük patted her head. "I thought you were smarter."

He handed her two bread rolls and a pat of butter. "Slim pickings again, but there might be some good leftovers tomorrow. There's another wedding tonight. And Cotillion."

He spread butter over his roll and threw the knife over his shoulder again.
    "If you were smart, you'd save the butter. You could use it to free yourself. I won't tell you how, but I've seen it done. You could sleep in the HVAC unit, nice and warm. Might be a good night for that, it's supposed to snow."

Cherry chewed half of her roll and saved the rest in her lap. She dug her nails into her palm hoping he wouldn't turn around and see the pearl necklace strewn past the fence. She didn't know why he was taunting her with the keys, goading her into finding the two dead girls.

He kicked her shin with his black non-slip shoe. "Quiet today."
  "I'm just cold."
  "27 degrees tonight. Bundle up!" He wrapped the tarp around her shoulders and pulled the edges around her neck, pushing her chin up to his. "Have a nice day, Cherry."

*

She tried every key to every door on the roof again, hoping she'd get inside. She was so cold she considered taking one of the tarps from the dead girls. She opened their door and unwrapped them. They were decomposing slowly in the cold. The redhead had a long deep cut down her shirt, from her ribs to her bellybutton. He had wrapped tinfoil around her torso to keep her organs in. It didn't work. Cherry wrapped her back up. The other girl was less decomposed and she could see that her wrists were slashed and her entire forehead was caved in. She wondered if the girl had found the redhead, and killed herself before Vük returned. Cherry locked the door behind her. She slept the rest of the day so she'd be awake for the night's freeze. It would be too easy to die in her sleep.

She jumped at the sound of Vük's door, her stomach strangled with fear that he'd notice the new tarps. She pushed them under her legs and pulled an old one up to her chin.

A preteen in a wrinkled blazer took off his dress shoe to use as a doorstop. Cherry couldn't find her voice and took off another necklace to throw at them. A second boy started running towards her yelling, *there's a girl up here.* The boy with one shoe offered her his phone while the other called the police. The screen couldn't sense her cold fingers.

The paramedic that put a foil blanket over Cherry heard her mumble *more girls on the roof.* The country club was evacuated, stranding dozens of wedding guests and a crying bride and confused teenage boys wondering if this was divine intervention saving them from Cotillion. They leaned over the caution tape and gaped at the body bags being carried out through the ballroom.

They were identified as Rosemary Lyman, 24, and Bela Diaz, 31. The Serbian was never found. He stole a catering van in the commotion of Cherry's discovery and peeled out without arousing suspicion. The van was found abandoned somewhere in Southern Ohio, his pinstripe vest and nametag neatly folded in the driver's seat.

Chapter IX. The Devil.
Ivan's Nightmare

- *Chapter III. The Confession Of A Passionate Heart—In Verse.
The Brothers Karamazov, p. 126*

I don't remember where I heard about the camera. Maybe through eavesdropping, or maybe it was one of my premonitions. Maybe I heard it while passing by one of the campus tour guides, although this is unlikely. I usually step off the sidewalk and cut through the grass whenever I see those red polos leading a sweaty herd of parents around the quad. But ever since I found out about the existence of a 24/7 live feed filmed from a webcam on the facade of Wallace Library I couldn't stop thinking about my Plan. There is only one acceptable use for such a camera.

I think about it with my feet on my desk watching my students watch *Mothlight*. I wonder if I'll be back here next week, teaching FILM 371, *Film and the Gaze*. Lacan, Mulvey, Sartre's lens-eye. My students come in a range of enthusiasm and aptitudes. Unfortunately, those attributes tend to be negatively correlated. The girl that always sits in the middle of the front row seems to never give her arm any rest. She always raises her hand and I always call on her immediately so I don't have to see that oval sweat spot. I dissociate during her sweaty, repetitive spiels about Shepitko and Varda. She chews the pleasure out of their films for me. She grinds them to dust with her big, overlapping teeth, teeth that look like she saved Warsaw in 1939 by trapping the Luftwaffe's bombs in her mouth. My eyes unfocus and I picture her as a wet, plastic, noisy juicer. I picture ripping her cord out of the wall. The fat kid next to her is the pile of pulp dumped into the sink. Citrus skin and banana peels and pureed spinach. Maybe that diet would do him some good. I picture him crawling around a pen, squealing with delight as I throw him an apple core. At least he gives me something to smile about—his undying loyalty to Michael Bay.

After class, a hippy walks into the graduate student lounge and passes me a petition imploring the film department to do something about the mold in the media studies building. I make her explain the neurological impacts of mycotoxins to me. Twice. Headaches, nosebleeds, nausea, tinnitus, muscle aches, sinusitis, respiratory issues, fainting spells, irritability. I can see her areolas through her crochet top. I sign my name, the secret one that I scribble everywhere I can: *Udo Erostratus*. Not Udo, as in Udo Kier[1], *Udo* as in *Udovolstviye*, the Russian word for Pleasure. *Erostratus* for the Greek who deigned to make a name for himself by burning down the second temple of Artemis. Fame through destruction. He was successful on both accounts. The Greeks impotently tried to invoke a *damnatio memoriae* law against him, forbidding anyone to speak or write his name. What good that did. He's still a legend, and not in the mythological sense.

Nastasia Polikarpovna, my RUSS 307 instructor, assigned us Book III of Brothers Karamazov, *The Sensualists*. I read it twice. Prostrate on my sheepskin rug, next to my pyramid of olives and champagne[2] on my mother of pearl tray, my hips idly pressed into the fur, Rostropovich spinning in the background, I declared myself a Sensualist as well.

A Sensualist is not merely a hedonist. A Sensualist is a man who is sentimental to the point of wickedness, a sanguine melancholy that becomes its own weather system. Pleasure, joy, and rage ferment inside his chest, to a level that can only be tempered with Education. He lives off poetry, film, lust, intoxication, music, and Pleasure. I get up to flip the record. Rostropovich's first name, Mstislav, means vengeance and glory. A Sensual name if I ever heard one.

---

1 I reject any association with Kier; a pederast in My Own Private Idaho, an expert of covens in Suspiria, a disembodied parodic German accent whenever he is needed for an animated children's cartoon.

2 "I'm not drinking, I'm only 'indulging,' as that pig, your Rakitin, says. He'll be a civil councilor one day, but he'll always talk about 'indulging.'" *Dmitri Karamazov, Chapter III. The Confession Of A Passionate Heart—In Verse, p. 126*

I like to work out with a little buzz going, late at night, when the people with jobs get their exercise. *How many guns could I buy with my $4,000/ semester TA stipend*, I wonder, as I look around the gym, riding the elliptical without breaking a sweat. I never sweat. I smell like bergamot oil and cologne delivered from a Russian bodega in Brighton,[3] *Troy-noy Odekolon*. Napoleon's own. The gym is disgusting but good people watching. In fact, I saw a celebrity here last week. An NFL quarterback who was filmed beating his pregnant fiancée in an elevator only days before.[4] The news cycle was fresh on his heels, not even a hint of a blue spore or a rancid scent wafting from the coverage of his assault. And yet here he was, in another elevator, holding a basketball. There was a fat brunette gym employee riding the elevator with us. She asked me to take a photo of them together. He signed the basketball for her and made her day. I feel short of breath and decrease my speed and think of my Plan and it soothes me.

> Take the green marble staircase to the second floor
> of the library, the busiest.
> Barricade the first and third floor doors, and prop
> open the second and fourth floors.
> Aim from the door, through the glass. Invisible.
>
> Aim at the cloisters of round tables, where people
> meet for group projects. It will be funny to see them
> scrambling to pretend they knew and cared about
> each other in the days after X.
>
> The fourth floor is always empty.
> Take one victim, as quietly as possible.
> Someone small, no more than 120 pounds.

---

3 Nastasia Polikarpovna hasn't said anything, but I saw her long fox nose twitch when I greeted her by her desk. I almost started to laugh, how easily I unlocked an olfactory Electric memory of her father. I bet she thought I was laughing at her body, her second-trimester bump she tries to hide under floral trapeze dresses.

4 The bird's eye angle of the elevator camera is very evocative. Filmed from above, women appear more diminutive and attractive, all you see is hair and cleavage and their impotent little fists waving in the air. The elevator camera sheds 40 pounds. That bird's eye view is really something.

The lighter the better.[5]

> Hang them from the neck with my ethernet cable,
> lowering them over the webcam, just so the top of
> their head is visible, so spectators can see the grassy
> mall, the picnics, the pillared academic buildings.
> So I can see the moment they all realize they're
> playing hangman.

I continue my subliminal warfare on Nastasia Polikarpovna, playing Swan Lake on my phone as she walks into the classroom. She looks around, trying to find the source of the Tchaikovsky. I'm trying to wake up a distant instinct. During the Soviet Union, radio and television stations would play Swan Lake on a loop during every uprising and putsch to jam the signals. The revolution wasn't televised, but at least you could enjoy a nice ballet.

Nastasia Polikarpovna, who I cannot refer to as Nastya, even in my mind, even when I am being a Sensualist on my sheepskin rug with the lotion and pillows, is especially flushed[6] today. It gives her face a hormonal Sensuality. It compliments her light brown hair, bright blue eyes, doll-like eyelashes and untouched eyebrows, full lips and delicate hands. Her toes swell in her sandals and she takes them off ten minutes after class begins. I heard she might go on maternity leave before the semester is over. We're only halfway through *Brothers*. I wish a snowstorm would throw us into a delay. Sometimes when she reads *Ivan Karamazov*[7] out loud she pauses and looks up at me with a little smirk.

I walk to the media studies building to teach my last class of the day. The Girl with the Gummo Tattoo is always early, sullen in her oversized hoodie in the middle row. She comes to class stoned and plagiarizes her essays. I let her pass regardless. I don't need to read every Harmony Korine Harley Quinn's opinion on Rohmer. The only student I have any

------

5 If they aren't so heavy, their body won't put too much strain on the neck, they won't die instantly. They'll wriggle around in front of the camera like a worm in an eagle's mouth. A worm who finally got to see the ocean.

6 "I shall be told, perhaps, that red cheeks are not incompatible with fanaticism and mysticism." *Chapter V. Elders, p. 26.*

7 Ivan is her name for me, a Russianization of John.

respect for in this classroom is Joel, the bug eyed accounting major who sits in the middle-center of the room next to her. I heard him mention he sits there for the ideal acoustics, but I wonder if it's because Gummo girl only wears pants if it gets below 45 degrees. Maybe he likes the way Zoe's thighs flatten onto her chair, the little bunny suit tattoo contracting and expanding as she fidgets. Maybe he likes the white scars that shred her thighs like shark gills. Maybe he's a Sensualist too.

I wake up on an invertebrate Saturday with nothing scheduled and go sit in the cafe waiting for one person, one voice, one sentence that could steer my mind away from the Plan.[8] But everyone is shrill and the saxophone of the elevator music is being drowned out by a little boy playing a small trumpet and Kaiser Permanente HR women on their laptops chewing chicken and waffles into their headsets. *Smack, smack, smack. No that won't be covered. No, that's not how we define 'emergency'.*

A pretty student is shoveling a croissant sandwich into her mouth. Her sundress is covered in crumbs and flakes and smudges of hot sauce. She wipes her mouth with a napkin more times than necessary and stands up to brush all her crumbs onto the floor. When she stands up, she instinctively smooths her dress from behind, running a hand along the backs of her thighs to make sure it hasn't gotten hiked up, to make sure my day will continue to be completely drab and void of beauty and Pleasure.

I wonder if it's best to abduct a woman after a large meal, or before she's eaten. There are good arguments for both possibilities. With the unfed woman, hunger is an effective bargaining chip. Her blood sugar is flatlining, she's desperate. She'll comply with any orders if I promise her a falafel. The satiated woman, on the other hand, does not want. But here's the rub— the hungry woman is alert, aroused, focused, and goal-oriented. The satiated woman is lethargic and dull. Women are truly slaves to their blood sugar. Especially now, in this world where a woman who is not suffering from insulin resistance is as rare as an albino crocodile. This question began to plague me. There is no way to answer it without experience, without experimentation. There is no literature on the matter. Maybe there is, but it's nothing I could look up without

---

8 "One can love one's neighbors in the abstract, or even at a distance, but at close quarters it's almost impossible." *Ivan K., Chapter IV. Rebellion, p. 297.*

receiving a visit from the campus Gestapo. They sent me a letter a few weeks ago, scolding me for pirating *The Sniper (1952)*.

"This property has been inspected by the Mercer County Department of…" a man reads the inspection certificate to his son, who has ceased his trumpeting. Somehow, this is worse.[9] Hearing him explain the minutiae of Food and Beverage bureaucracy to his son breaks my back. I suck down the rest of my drink through the sogging paper straw and return to campus to bloodlet my incurable graphomania and write two confessions.[10] The first was more general, a simple manifesto and explanation of the Plan. The second one was for Nastasia. Because I am thirteen rungs above her on the ladder[11], I couldn't bear to use my own words on her. I took a pair of scissors to my copy of *Brothers*, God forgive me, to save myself from the labor of writing. Recently my fingers and wrists have grown numb: pins and needles. My vision is blurring, and I have found it hard to write or even type at length. My patience, for months, has been deteriorating, ever since I took the teaching position. My *joie de vivre* is fading with each moment here, in New Jersey, amongst these lazy students who mar the Princeton reputation. It seems I have extracted the essence of all of life's Pleasure that has been made available to me.

Dear Nastasia Polikarpovna,

Why have I been longing for you? Why have I been
thirsting for you all these days, and just now? Because
it's only to you I can tell everything; because I must,

---

9 "I knew a criminal in prison who had, in the course of his career as a burglar, murdered whole families, including several children. But when he was in prison, he had a strange affection for them. He spent all his time at his window, watching the children playing in the prison yard. He trained one little boy to come up to his window and made great friends with him." *Ivan K., Chapter IV. Rebellion, p. 298.*

10 "Confession is a great sacrament, before which I am ready to bow down reverently; but there in the cell, they all kneel down and confess aloud. Can it be right to confess aloud? It was ordained by the holy Fathers to confess in secret: then only your confession will be a mystery, and so it was of old." *Ivan K., Chapter VIII. The Scandalous Scene, p. 106.*

11 "I wasn't blushing at what you were saying or at what you've done. I blushed because I am the same as you are." "You? Come, that's going a little too far!" "No, it's not too far," said Alyosha warmly (obviously the idea was not a new one). "The ladder's the same. I'm at the bottom step, and you're above, somewhere about the thirteenth. That's how I see it. But it's all the same. Absolutely same in kind. Anyone on the bottom step is bound to go up to the top one." *Alyosha K. Chapter IV. The Confession Of A Passionate Heart—In Anecdote, p. 133.*

because I need you, because to-morrow I shall fly from the clouds, because to-morrow life is ending and beginning. Have you ever felt, have you ever dreamt of falling down a precipice into a pit? That's just how I'm falling, but not in a dream. And I'm not afraid, and don't you be afraid. At least, I am afraid, but I enjoy it. It's not enjoyment though, but ecstasy. Damn it all, whatever it is! A strong spirit, a weak spirit, a womanish spirit—whatever it is![12]

Prashai,
Ivan

*

On Monday, I tucked the letters into my laptop bag and walked to the media studies building. My last class. I buzzed with relief and excitement and walked faster than usual, holding doors, smiling at women, and letting drivers pass before marching down the crosswalk. I even began to sweat. I'd worn my houndstooth wool blazer, the most attractive piece of clothing I own, albeit inappropriate for the season.

I stood in front of my class realizing I'd forgotten my lesson plan. I forgot which film I was showing the students, which reading to summarize. I looked through my laptop bag for a clue. Then I woke up to my students standing over me, my shirt unbuttoned, my papers strewn about.

"Zoe just gave you CPR," Joel beamed. That explained the faint smell of cannabis and chapstick on my breath.
   "Thank you, Zoe."

I get up and fall down again, my forehead almost slamming into my desk. Joel and Zoe caught me before I could complete my crash landing. Joel rolls my office chair towards me and lowers me in. There is bright, fresh blood all over my papers. Zoe begins to collect them in a pile, presumably for the trash. I try to stop her, but the credits roll again.

---

12 *Chapter III. The Confession Of A Passionate Heart—In Verse, p. 126.*

I wake up laying across the backseat of a car. The sun is pouring in through the window above me; I feel myself spinning, a zoetrope. The sun shines through trees and buildings and powerlines. Joel is driving. His car is messier than I expected.

"Zoe let me borrow her car." That explains it. "She couldn't come with us, she has therapy after film class."

"Where are you driving to?"

"The hospital. I called the health center and they said they can't take you, they don't do emergencies."

I sat up so quickly I saw stars. "I don't have health insurance. Take me back to campus, to my apartment. No hospitals." I laid back down using Zoe's CD case as a pillow.

*

I took three sick days. I watched movies and slept and made finger sandwiches and ate the rest of my olives. I went through half of my vinyl collection until I couldn't bear to listen to music through my pulsating migraine. I got so bored I turned on the Wallace Library livestream and let it run. I watched the campus for hours, the various waves of migration across the lawn. The Unstaged, The Fortuitous, Endlessness, The Indeterminate, The Flow of Life. I almost fell asleep before catching a pair of thighs appearing in front of the camera, white and hairless and marked and flailing. I saw the bunny tattoo and corn-silk scars and clutched the sides of my laptop. Zoe had stolen my letters, my plan, my vengeance, my glory. She had burned down my temple and turned my dreams to ashes. I may have plagiarized my suicide note but she plagiarized her own suicide.

I called 911 as I ran to the Wallace Library to cut her down.

Some Like it Orange

Oksana left the rock climbing center after finding out she didn't get the job. The manager was kind about it. He offered her an iced tea from the employee lounge and told her to come back for another drug test in two months.

"Some things stay in your system longer than you know."

She walked outside and sipped the tea on a bench nearby, wondering if she was supposed to take the bus home or cross the street to Dougherty's for a drink. She gravitated towards the wood-paneled watering hole like a dowser. She felt eyes on her in the bar and chalked it up to the Lululemons she'd taken from the lost and found that were cut to make skinny asses like hers have the curve of a string instrument. Her collarbone-length bleached hair had the opalescent tinge of a pale green dye job from three months ago. Her eyes were upturned but narrow, shrinking under the dark swell of yesterday's eyeliner that inflamed her lids. Her high cheekbones held pools of dark circles, low iron and bad sleep.

Craig left five minutes after her, still in his rock climbing outfit, blue shorts that ended mid thigh, leg muscles like he was smuggling something in his calves. Long torso, short limbs, short curly hair. He kept it buzzed on the sides and a little longer on top to hide his mid-30's thin-out. He had marble eyes, sea-green like a cat's, two clocks over his perfect teeth, tightly packed from a humiliating stretch of adult orthodontia.

When she saw him walk into the bar she remembered she was supposed to wait for him on that bench. *Stay put.* She wondered if she was supposed to feel ashamed, if she had embarrassed him by failing the drug

44

test again, or if a pool of black ash in her gut was making it all up. In her mind, the oven was always on, the water always left running, and the door was always unlocked.

He slid onto a stool next to hers in his little blue shorts. "Found you."

She liked the way he put his sweater around her, a fleece half-zip that smelled like detergent.

"We only drink at home, Oksana. Remember? There are toxins in the drinks here, it interacts with your medicine."

"I didn't get the job."

"I know, Justin told me."

"Are you upset with me?"

"Not at all. I'm proud of you for trying."

*

One day he came home with a baby wrapped in white blankets and a little green hat. He offered the swaddled mass to her, then laid the baby on the couch when her arms stayed frozen to her sides.

"I noticed you've been bored lately. Maybe it gets lonely here while I'm away. Vimal and his wife are going on vacation for two weeks and I told them you could watch their son while they're in Miami."

She looked at the couch, saw the mess of blankets, the baby peering out, and walked out into the Boston winter with no keys, no phone, and no coat.

Three days later, she woke up in her bed with the vague memory of being kicked off a train. There was no baby and no Craig in the apartment. She was naked and her hair was still wet, freshly washed, smelling like her apple shampoo. Her muscles had that bleached, weak, dehydrated feeling, like she'd been drinking on the outside. There were bruises on her arms and shins. Her knees were scraped, but the wounds were clean. One of them even looked half healed.

The TV was on in the living room. A continuous 5-minute loop of a cartoon she watched as a little kid. A little brown mammal with satellite-dish ears was fast asleep in a box of oranges. She turned off the TV and looked for something sweet.

The refrigerator was full of her favorite yogurt that Craig ordered by subscription. Every week, a 12-pack of strawberry-banana yogurt shipped in dry ice would appear outside their door. She peeled the foil top off and the smell brought back a recent memory of vomiting up bananas on rain-soaked concrete.

She remembered some things:
    standing in line in grade school,
    being scolded for eating chalk,
    holding out her tongue for iodine drops,
    wading in the Black Sea until the sand gave way,
    a flounder swimming out from under her feet.

She took two more showers and ate five more yogurts while she waited for Craig to come home. She wondered if she'd remember something if she kept tasting banana.

*

"Why did you ask me to take care of your coworker's baby?"

"Vimal's kid is 4 now. You met him for 5 seconds at the office Christmas party when he was 7 months old. His wife tried to put the baby in your arms and you just stood there, not moving your arms, until you left to go soak your feet in the fountain."

"There was a baby here on the couch."

Craig wrapped his arms around her and smelled her thrice washed damp hair. Her dark roots were pushing further and further down, the green tinge had almost disappeared from her bleached waves.

"I'm gonna get you an appointment at the salon tomorrow. Let's make you blonder. And once it gets warm again, I'll take you to the beach. Promise."

She stood stiff, barefoot on cold tile, too confused to relax into his arms, too guilty to accept them.

*

Last year a journalist visited McLean Hospital to ask about a patient who had been discharged last year. She found Oksana playing with a chessboard, peeling the felt pads off each piece.

"I don't remember her."

"She was a teenager, an anorexic. They put her in the Celexa trial. You would have seen her every day."

She held up a photo of a group of women standing in a row, holding up paper valentines. She pointed to Oksana at the end of the row, then a blonde girl standing next to her.

"I've never seen her before in my life. I'd remember that forehead anywhere."

"Michelle needs your help. She's going on trial for her friend's death, they're saying she provoked him to suicide. Can I record you telling me how the medicine makes you feel? How you forget things, how you don't feel quite yourself?"

Oksana stuck eight felt pads to her fingertips and slid her hands around the chess board.

"The passcode to the old people ward is written inside the leaves of a drawing under the lightswitch at the end of the hallway. You can type the numbers into the door and steal their oranges."

*

Her cheek felt so good against the cold window. February frost etched cracks onto the glass that would melt soon, no real damage, just the illusion. Protesters were gathered seventeen floors below her.

"Did you drive past them on your way home? What do their signs say?"

"Didn't notice. For some people, protesting is a hobby. It's just what they do."

"Just what they do," she repeated. "What do you do, Craig? I can't remember."

"I'm a consultant."

"What does that mean?"

"People consult with me on decisions for their companies and we contract work to other…"

She fell back onto the bed. He was saying words that meant something, if you held them to the light, if you passed that test, if you'd studied for it, if you were paying attention that day. She was too tired to listen, her bed wasn't white enough, there wasn't a button she could press that would make it bend under her knees. She'd had one of those before, she couldn't remember where. Craig gave her something warm and acidic to drink, bright blue in a white mug.

"I made you something, just how you like it."

"I like it when you turn the stove off," she whispered into his curls.

He straddled her on the bed, fixing the angle of her neck before he pulled her collarbone into a kiss. "I love your Dostoevsky tattoo."

«сознавать — это болезнь»
Consciousness is an illness

She didn't remember telling him what that tattoo read. She didn't remember telling him about any of the tattoos she'd gotten as a preteen, anything about that decade she'd spent huffing glue on the banks of the Dnieper, earning money in a way that would make Kuprin blush.

"Kirilis translated for me." He bit the strap of her tank top and peeled it down to her elbow.

She didn't remember Craig's Latvian coworker ever being close enough to see the script on her chest, an area she kept covered up around strangers on account of her implanted access port, a bruisey lump over her heart.

"When did he see it?"

"He saw a picture."

*

Craig kept his promise. On Memorial Day, he rented a beach house in Narragansett for Oksana and three of his coworkers.

"Why aren't their girlfriends here too?"
  "Because they have wives, not girlfriends."

She woke up to the sound of Craig and the other men playing an evening poker game. She ran into the Latvian in the kitchen, saw him reach into the fridge and drink from her glass bottle, the one Craig mixed just for her. He didn't like her drinking beer, wine, hard liquor, or anything they sold in bars. *No sulfites*, he explained.

"Then what's in it?" Kirilis asked, giving it another smell. "Kombucha? Vermouth?"

She took a swig and asked if he wanted to get into the ocean with her.

"I heard you're a strong swimmer," he smirked.

Kirilis had heard about Providence. He'd heard about how Oksana came to Rhode Island when she was 22 years old, flown from Ukraine with a truckload of other Slavs to work as lifeguards up and down the East Coast; Hilton Head to Ocean City crawling with Bulgarians and Russians.

She worked the pool of a motel, an easy job, only a 7 foot deep end. She could see the ocean from her roost. She made extra money from the motel guests until she got caught letting a 14 year old boy come of age inside her for $50. A beach cleaner had found them at dawn, sleeping on the sand. Oksana's bathing suit and clothes had been swept away by the high tide.

She was held in Providence until a guard saw her eating crumbs of plaster from the walls of her jail cell. RIDOC transferred her to a psych hold in Massachusetts. At McLean, she was put on concurrent and consecutive drug trials. Two years into her stay, a pharmaceutical consultant leaving a meeting noticed her sunbathing in the garden. One month later, she was released into Craig's custody.

Oksana and Kirilis walked down the staircase of the big white beach house down to the water. Pebbles, rocks, coarse sand, and driftwood hurt the bottoms of their feet. She stripped and weighed her clothes down with a heavy rock. He tread water next to her, his pupils dilated, reflecting the full moon back at her.

"I can barely move my legs. What's in that stuff he's been giving you? No wonder you're always barely coherent."

"If it's hard to swim, just stop resisting and float on your back."

The moon was so bright she hoped it would give her a tan.
    So bright she could feel it above her with her eyes closed.

She felt Kirilis leading her somewhere, telling her things that could get her in trouble. The cold salt water felt so good she couldn't tell if she was supposed to be ashamed or scared, if she had done something wrong or if he was tricking her. Four blue-orange gas flames began to simmer in her chest.

"That's your money. Disability, unemployment, the drug trials…he's got a little scheme going. And that's not even including what he makes off your *videos*…Do you ever get scared?"

*

"She must be over 18, look at all her tattoos."
    "I've had these since I was 12."
    "What's your date of birth?"
    "There's no school on my birthday."
    "When's your birthday?"
    "My boyfriend is an Aries."

Oksana felt her wheelchair switch hands. The second person pushed faster and whipped around the hospital corridors. A different woman's voice was behind her head, asking questions and dialing a phone.

"Your boyfriend's coming. He's outside talking to the police."
    "We were supposed to go to the beach…"

"Do you know where you are, ma'am?"

"But then Kirilis hit his head on a rock. Or wait— that's not it. We couldn't go to the beach because I don't have a bathing suit. Mine got sucked into the ocean when I was a lifeguard."

"You're in Rhode Island, honey. In the hospital. You're not a lifeguard. You just tried to save your friend, the one who hit his head, but he didn't make it. Has anyone told you that yet?"

She woke up with Craig nestled beside her, forehead to cheekbone in white flannel hospital blankets.

"Is Kirilis still out there, swimming around, looking for my bathing suit?"

"He is."

"He said a lot of things out there, when we were in the ocean together."

"You told me an hour ago, before you fell asleep."

"I took care of it."

"I didn't know you could do something like that."

"Are you upset with me?"

He kissed her forehead four times, turning off every burner one by one.

The Taco Bell in the Center of the Pentagon

"The Three Disgraces!" Olamide yelled across the hotel pool. "Beauty, elegance...mirth."

He carried his shoes as he walked towards the hot tub, muttering virtues to himself. Mila sank her shoulders underwater, crossing her arms over her chest. Ksenia rolled her elbows back onto the rim, doubling down.

"I should be a medium. A psychic. I should read palms in a strip mall, like a gypsy." He breathed heavily as his big feet slapped against the tiles. He said this is the last time he catches us topless and drunk off Henny and hot tub fumes after hours. He said that if we were his daughters, he would be in prison. I've seen his daughters. I've seen their yellow eyes, their knock knees, calves splayed out in an X. *Jiminy rickets.* Growing up in basements, hidden away from the equatorial sun.

"Last time, we *promise*." Ksenia offered him a drink. The diplomat. In 24 hours, she'd be proven right. I watched his hand dwarf the amber bottle and got a feeling. A greedy feeling that we were going to run out and the demon seed would gnaw on my soul with its yellow rodent teeth unless I poisoned it to sleep.

There's war on the border. Not this one. The other one. *Someone shot a plane down over Donetsk,* Mila had texted me. *My flights have been canceled for the week. I'll text you when I get on the shuttle from Dulles.*

"Ten minutes. I'll be checking the cameras."
"Those cameras don't work. The only real cameras are behind reception,

52

in the gift shop, and—"

Someone kicked me underwater. Probably the diplomat.

The three of us reeked of chlorine and Angel, the only perfume to persevere through hours of nightswimming. Our six legs in a row, breaching in and out of the froth, were pink from the hot steam. We stained three towels and the bath mat when we dyed my hair that morning. Some kind of brown-black from CVS. 'Velvet Cardamom', 'Midnight Macadamia' or something. I couldn't stop playing with my new braids. I love the shiny, heavy feeling of freshly dyed hair, a new glassy sheath around every strand, unfamiliarly contrasting against my skin.

I was the last Disgrace still working at the rooftop bar atop the Pentagon Marriott. Mila quit to work for Aeroflot. Olamide fired Ksenia a month ago for smoking behind the bar. She always smoked up there. It calmed her fear of heights. One day she ashed into a woman's fish and chips. *"I thought she was done! Slow eater."* She never needed the job anyway. She has an entire room just for clothes in her adoptive parents' five story house near Chevy Chase Circle. She bartends until she gets fired or quits or decides to travel. It doesn't bother me much. She's a slippery koi in a heated pond. Why should she suffer? It's not her fault she was too young to remember her plastic cup on the pet store shelf.

Mila had to sell her mother's opal earrings to make enough money to leave Brooklyn when her adoptive parents found out she was 22, not 17. She thought she'd find someone sympathetic in Brighton, the Russian dollhouse slapped together by bitter immigrants in the Fascist 40s. Where tourists swish around a replica of the Nylon 90s. Where expats spit between their Nike slides and swear they'll never return to Eastern Ashtray, while they fully recreate it on every block. She left Ischild Jewelry & Watch Repair with $150 and a Rockville address. The jeweler told her to go check on his niece *who never calls* and ask her for a job.

Back in the hotel room, we passed around a bottle of grenache I stole from the roof and watched TV in our king bed. I swore I saw a glimpse of Braveheart— Ksenia was flipping through channels looking for Mel. A man was stuffing dryer sheets into his wife's mouth on Lifetime. She lingered on it for a bit and started to laugh. Mila threw a tissue box at the TV and growled for a channel change in Russian. Ksenia ignored her, like always, sensitive about her monolingualism. Mila grabbed the remote. Their quiet rivalry was flaring up and I slid deeper under our big white comforter.

She flipped through channels hungrily, barely giving anything a breath, until she saw a cross legged Buddhist engulfed by flames on Discovery. Mila grabbed the bottle, still hoarding the remote, and told us about the last time she ever saw her mother alive. They were riding the bus, right after the default. She doesn't remember what her mother was saying or how she looked that morning. She was watching a Korean man self immolating with paper rubles and *samogon*.

Her mother bought fake documents to knock five years off her age and get her into one of the best boarding schools in Moscow. It closed after three years and she transferred to mine, an Orthodox boarding school for priests' children and orphans in Podmoskovye. On her first day, I stole her gold and opal earrings during gym so no one else would. I gave them back to her later that night and taught her where to hide things and who to hide them from. We whispered until 2 AM and our friendship had been mostly nocturnal ever since.

I dragged her out to the balcony to cool off.

Our view faced the highway, Reagan Airport, and the Potomac. Cars, planes, and the river breathed movement into a city with notoriously bad circulation. Humidity and red tape. Gua sha over concrete.

Ola was kind enough to let his Disgraces have one of the nice rooms for free, the ones blocked off for week-long conferences. Balconies and king beds to jack up the cost, gringo prices for the federal government.

"What if I was in that plane that got shot down."
　　"That would *never* happen to an Aeroflot vessel."
　　She saluted the river and laughed.
　　"Malaysia Airlines is really having some bad luck this year. Aren't Asians supposed to be the luck experts?"
　　"Maybe they're obsessed with luck, because they've never had it."
　　"Alan Watts. Law of negative. Too many fortune cookies and joy luck clubs."

"As if Russians aren't the most superstitious people on the planet."

"We are. But *blessed are those who mourn—*"

"Do you ever get used to flying?"

"No. The only time I pray anymore is during takeoff and landing. *Lord save and protect me, a sinner.*" She crossed herself.

"When you die in a plane crash, do you suffocate midair, or do you die on impact?"

"It depends on the speed of deceleration. Eyeballs out, eyeballs in…"

"What are you two talking about?" Ksenia spanked me with the remote. "*Signs* is on."

I slept until noon the next day, the first one up. I wanted them to come make work bearable. But M+K take forever to get ready. I tried to button Mila's stewardess uniform onto her stiff body and recreate her velvet-matte mile-high makeup. She always traveled with her little Aeroflot portable mirror and nylon mesh travel bag sitting in a crescent on the laminated desk. Three perfume bottles standing in front of their boxes like prom dates. Nude stockings and her silk airline scarf hanging over the rolling chair. Two Aeroflot uniforms in orange and blue. I could never remember which one she was wearing on any given day. They seemed identical to me, like a negative photo, or a sun-blinded glance. She was one of those people who checks into a hotel and actually uses the dresser, actually hangs her clothes up in the closet, and might even break out the ironing board. I live out of backpacks that crouch in the corner.

The bed creaked under my knees and makeup brushes spilled out of my apron onto our bed with a small racket. Ksenia grumbled and twisted in her sleep. Concealer oozed over our sheets. I twisted Mila's silk scarf with my index and picked up her tiny bleached head to snake it behind her throat and around. I tied it under her chin with two tails flowing to the right, tighter until her eyes flicked open and she bucked me off the bed onto rough carpet. I stayed there for a moment, winded, staring at the ceiling. I opened the mini fridge with my big toe and cooled my feet against a row of aluminum cans.

"Next time I'm this hungover, drown me in the bath like a kitten." Mila stepped over me to get a shower beer. After a few minutes I heard her smash a can against the tiles like a Camry. I stretched on the floor dreading work, dreading the rooftop. Mila promised she'd wake up before 2 and come entertain me.

"You made my eyes look so beady!" She washed off the makeup I carefully brushed onto her little green eyes. I'd dabbed concealer onto her nose, cheeks, and chin, the parts of her face that get pink after she's had a few. The stewardess uniform that took so long to fasten onto her was crumpled on the carpet.

I went back to work, flinching at every flash of blue and orange in my peripheral vision, waiting for Mila to show up, one foot in front of the other, knees almost knocking, pencil skirt trapping her gait like a belt buckled around her thighs. She loves wearing her uniform off duty.

"Her uniform is so gauche," Ksenia would say, rolling her eyes. "Watch her eat it up."

"You don't seem to mind when it gets us free rounds."

Jack gave me a ticket as soon as I got upstairs and warned me about a busy night. Some DOD conference. He was working an Asian woman reading at the bar. Red glasses and long straight hair. Five olives in her martini. He was leaning too far forward, she wasn't making eye contact.
  "Guess it's not *that* busy," I grumbled in earshot.
  "Could be worse, some of them are partying in their rooms. They like their privacy."
  I backed off. He'd be occupied for a while, and I could easily sneak away after an hour. There's something sweet about a reluctant yet captive audience. Being ignored really sticks to the ribs.

Every night I was surrounded by slick mouths and stained teeth and flushed cheeks. The sun was going down and the empties were stacking up and the mouths were opening wider and wider. Whenever I bring the mouths their drinks, I catch whiffs of mildew, yeast, stillness, emptiness, and neuroticism that goes everywhere except into a box of floss. I moved aside a basket of fries to set down Striped Polo's fifth beer and when he *thaaanks* me I could see that his tongue was stark white. A carpeted closet. Candida swarming around his gut with power tools.

Have you ever watched incense burn from across the room, given a little gust of breath in its direction, and watched how the smoke bristles and dances, how you've changed the current of all the air in the room without leaving your bed?

Ever scattered a flock of seagulls with one stomp?

I pick someone to stare at for too long until their chin drops to check their front. They look down to check for spills and pinch their shirts to loosen it up over their guts. *Telekinesis.*

Jack is always upselling the beers here so he doesn't have to mix drinks. They're all 'easy drinking'. I scratch a tally into my itchy palm every time I hear his tagline. I wish he would try pretending not to hear the *guests*. I just nod and pour rail vodka sodas and shift my weight. Humans are so reluctant to confront. Men are so reluctant to disappoint women. They nod once, shrink their necks into their chests, and go back to their tables holding that little black napkin underneath that little clear drink they didn't ask for.

My back always hurts.

Sometimes the rooftop din starts to shoot through my shoulders and neck until my veins harden with black sludge.

I get impulsive
I get greedy
I hit cruise control
I think of money
Cloth-paper in my mind
Cotton-linen in my hands
A stack of bills folded like sedimentary rock down a highway
I once heard someone call it
Coyote blasting
I look for unattended boyfriends and unsupervised husbands
They buck at the mercy of my attention span
I hide their tips in my apron
Turn and shift into neutral

The keycard I stole from housekeeping hasn't been working so I've been more of a hunter than a gatherer this week. But sometimes these moods send me into the elevator, down into the corridors of the hotel. I would only steal from rooms with the door hanger turned to Do Not Disturb.

Those coy things. Wish they would just print ones that say *I don't want spics touching my shit, thanks, have a nice day.* Or *please don't knock because I'll think you're a cop or my wife and you'll have to scrape my corpse off the sidewalk.* I check jackets and coats for cash, and if I find a fanny pack, well, you have no idea how much people entrust to those things.

Downstairs with a handle of whiskey in my waistband. Passed 805 and I already heard Mila scolding someone. Her *shut off all electronic devices* voice. A hint of something Transatlantic lived beneath the Slavic accent, a remnant of learning English from perfumed and powdered lace collared Russians. Drunkenness draped a fur coat over her stuffy boarding school diction.

The housekeeping cart and Mila were blocking the doorframe but I squeezed through. A short barrel-shaped woman in a blue apron hurried past me and Mila threw something heavy at the bed, whining about being robbed.

"Yeah, no shit. Trying to rob you of your dirty towels."
I flipped the door hanger to *Do Not Disturb.*
In smaller font: *No Molestan.* Heh.

I sat by the desk, smelling her perfumes and listening to the little clicks of their smooth glass lids. The heavy purple Givenchy bottle, *Ange ou Demon,* is my favorite. The atomizer stares at me like a lens whenever I douse my neck and jawline with tuberose. I tied her scarf over my head like an executioner's hood and breathed in the musky vanilla silk as I fell back onto the bed next to her. Boozy sweat rose from the synthetic fabric of her uniform. The something heavy dug into my back. A crystal whiskey glass that wasn't the kind we use on the roof.
"Where'd you get this?"

She whimpered that she got too drunk with some guys Ksenia met on our floor and lost her keycard and hadn't eaten all day.

I took the pins out of her blonde chignon and braided her back into a sleepy civilian. She whispered gratitude into the pillow, one side of her pink and black makeup rubbing off onto white. A cheaper hotel would charge you for that.

"Come eat something upstairs." I tried to lift her off the bed. Her pink mouth went slack as a baby in the backseat. I searched her pockets and purse for a keycard and gave up and left the door propped open by the deadbolt.

"Hello? *Hola?*"

A refrigerator-sized man called to me from down the hall near the water fountain. He was sweating through his button down, swaying. His disproportionately small feet were splayed apart. He was built like a claw foot tub. He swung his big red bottle upside down and sucked it like a calf. The bottle's empty squeal pleaded against the squeeze of his grip.

He blocked my path and squeezed the bottle in my face again. And again. Close enough to smell his sweet stink and dissect the laminate swinging from his neck. A smaller version of his face gaped at me, trout lips hooked by a lanyard: *Asher Cohn.* Another defense contractor. I've never seen anyone DOD who I could trust around a freshly baked pie. I can only wonder how huge these guys would be if they could smoke weed.

"No trabajo." he pointed to the fountain, catching his breath, all heavy o's and r's. The drunken shrillness of his voice made me grind my teeth.
   "It hardly ever works. You can call someone to refill your mini fridge."
   "I'm not paying for *water.*"
   "Try the one by the gym."
   "I saw you looking at me on the roof."

I got a last glimpse of him as the elevator closed. What remained on his head was thinning, spat upon by the triumph of the hair gurgling up from his neck and back. His socks and belt cut into his body the way Mila's fingers were clutching her pillow in drunken slumber.
With my black hair, hoops, and apron staring back at me in the elevator door, maybe I did look Latina.

The supply closet on the 14th floor has jars of pickles, hot dog buns, and clear boxes full of ketchup and mayo packets. HEINZ HELLMAN'S HEINZ pressed up against the plastic. I figured that with the correct posture, I'll look like I'm working as I head back to the room with my loot.

There's something comforting about the smell of bleach. Even animals are drawn to it, I've noticed. The janitors have a boxy little TV in here that's always on. Always on cop show reruns. Dull, milky 90's blacks. Those grey-green dried out marker blacks, asphalt and detective coats the color of my apron. I've never seen this TV without a layer of cashmere dust. Cobblers and children and so on.

I slumped into the camping chair behind the shelf of plastic cups and cocktail napkins, swaddled by thick green canvas. I settled in to watch John or Tom get clipped on his morning run. Only *I* saw it happen. *Viewers like you.*

His scent calls upon the attention of a dog walker's tight-leashed terrier: blood and sweat and I'm guessing Acqua de Giò, the rest of which remains in a bathroom cabinet in Bethesda. I think about the free apartment. Cardboard boxes and permanent markers.

If you peeled down his collar you'd see the tag of his bloodstained crewneck sweatshirt boasting ring-spun cotton, authentic Hanes, American-made. It's generous in the shoulders and nipped at the wrists. As seen on Jerry and Diana and the feather-haired blonde families who wear them tucked in.

Zoom to a drop on his styrofoam-white Reeboks, a little red pearl you could pick up with tweezers.
Pan to his tennis-toned calves sticking out of the kudzu, Kennedy parted hair resting on dry leaves.
Cops have started to swarm Rock Creek. I count their big blue jackets like sheep.

In the countryside, I imagine, you can stash a letter in the knot of a tree for your lover and know he'll find it. He'll brush off the dirt and ants with his rough hands. He'll tuck it safely into the breast pocket of his big practical coat and smile on the walk back to his truck.

In the city, nothing is ever how you left it. There's no telling how many hands could have touched it, photographed it, stolen it.

You can't expect a stewardess in a hotel room propped open by the deadbolt to be exactly how you left her.

I sensed a stink familiar to me from a few hours ago. A sickly sweet humid smell that could only emit from a man's sweat glands or a pile of vomit. Strawberry banana smoothie left in a hot, musty, cloth seat car.

The lobby was swarming with police. Olamide told me to go back upstairs and find Ksenia. The paramedics ignored me too, busy keeping people from going outside to look. I knew the other exits.

More paramedics were standing around a tarp on the sidewalk. One of the cab drivers lining the street told me a girl jumped. He saw the whole thing.

"Was she wearing blue?"

"Maybe orange. Too dark to tell. You think you knew her?"

I ran back into the hotel through the exit I'd propped open with my balled up apron. Our room didn't face the cabs. It faced the highway. Olamide wanted the cops to leave as soon as possible. I could tell by the way he turned his ear to them.

I spent the night alone in our hotel room. Ksenia wouldn't answer her phone. She probably saw the cops and cut out. Back to Chevy Chase, back to her nest. I kept the TV on and took three showers. I couldn't sleep more than five minutes at a time. Her nude stockings scared me awake. They looked like a broken arm hanging off the chair. I balled them up and boxed the perfume.

The next day, I packed up all of Mila's things and took the bus to Rockville.

Apartment 716: Zinaida Ischild. A name so Jewish my teeth hurt. Sucking lemons sitting Shiva. I've never come here by myself. Whenever I dig my chipped nail polish into this buzzer, Mila's right behind me, her hands busy with a delivery of groceries and paper products. The first time I came here, I expected an old lady in an apartment full of doilies, not a young Barbra Streisand lookalike.

The air in Zina's apartment was always heavy with incense, smoke, and fried food. The smell hit me as she opened the door in her blush robe, scolding me until I took my shoes off. I gave her my ugly no-slip shoes and told her about Mila in a run-on apology for coming over empty handed. Her nose, cheeks, and chest burned pink. She sat down and hugged one of her beaded pillows, rocking cross legged on the big pink couch. She threw the pillow on the Persian rug and pulled me into her arms. I rested my chin on her cinnamon roots, parted in the middle, growing out, pushing against the bleach. Her head smelled sweet and oily like the croissants the hotel puts out for breakfast. I pulled away first and wiped the bottom of my face with my sleeve. I pulled one of Mila's perfumes out of my backpack and offered it to her.

"I'll never be able to wear this. But it'll look beautiful on my vanity."

She pulled the cigar box from under the coffee table and rolled us a joint with her long nails. I pictured Mila pulling her head back, crinkling her nose and fanning my smoke, reminding us how often she gets drug tested. She always perched a little further away, on the big red ottoman, drinking red wine out of a mug and licking it off her teeth before speaking. She never drank out of anything clear. "Plausible deniability." Zina whispered to me once. "My babushka was an alcoholic, always drank out of a plastic Disney world cup. Anything opaque, say it was sweet tea."

The tree loosened me up and I was able to stop crying and tell her about the bad smell, the wrong window, the man in the hallway. "He saw me leave her alone in our room. He watched me get on the elevator and then went in and took her. He needs to be dealt with. Disfigured. Discarded. Disposed of. He is not capable of anything better. He cannot control himself. He needs to be shot between the eyes like a 10 year old Golden Retriever."

She looked past my eyes with blank pity. "When was the last time you took a shower? Let me braid your hair."

I watched our reflection as her bent fingers ran over my scalp, gently parting my hair, like a bee collecting nectar. Her nails were hard and slippery with polish.

"You are very beautiful, if you look closely. Pity about that waitress uniform. And who talked you into this dye job? Black is too harsh for your complexion."

When I started to cry again Z patted my head and went back into the kitchen. I heard the refrigerator door swing open, bottles clinking. I heard screw top wine get poured into two glasses. I heard a heavier, porcelain-like chink on the counter and then I heard her put it back.

After a few hours, we were crossfaded and indiscreet, listening with our shoulders and speaking with our hands. She's a chatterbox bouncing on her haunches. I'm splayed out on the various embroidered pillows she keeps on the floor. The hem of her robe has disappeared into the cleavage of her big pale thighs.

"Women are rock, and men are sand…that's why they call it the sand-man… and you're an island. Picture Shutter Island, where's the sand? Just waves crashing forever, water to rock, and all you can do is be cute, aloof, unaffected, with a short memory….rock has the longest memory of anything on earth. You can point to a stripe from a million years ago, a primordial grudge. We fossilize shit. Have you been to El Dorado National Park? It's divine…have you been getting your beauty sleep? Sometimes, we get too sandy…what's the word? Sedimental…it dams our rivers…obscures perception, whittles you to a trickle, dials you down to your most basic instinct….til you can't do anything but curl up somewhere safe and sleep...your eyes are so red…"

Zina's analogy almost made sense to me so I took a swig of pink wine from the bottle while she rummaged in the bathroom.

She pulled the childproof lid off of a bottle of eyedrops and weaved her fingers through the base of my braid.

"Let me do it so you don't ruin your makeup."

"Don't get any in my mouth."

My lids shot open in epiphany and Zina scolded me for wasting her Systane. Tears, artificial and otherwise, scattered down my cheeks. In the balcony door's reflection I could see mascara hitching a liquid ride to my chin.

"I figured it out, Z. Jews don't do autopsies. It's against your religion. Right?"

"Rewind."

"We poison him."

She cocked an eyebrow. "How feminine. With what? Arsenic?"

"Eyedrops."

"I saw that Forensic Files."

"It could work. Are we going to hell?"

"We don't believe in hell. Just let him eat himself to death." She poured us another glass. "You ever meet a healthy Jew over 40?"

*

The service was in an Episcopalian church; all three Orthodox cathedrals refused to hold a funeral for a suicide. A Russian stewardess leapt out of an 8th floor balcony in a drunken stupor. Case closed.

Her hair was parted to the side to hide a large contusion on her forehead. Someone had dressed her in a starchy white shirt and slacks. They'd brushed dark eyeshadow on her lids and heavy blush on her cheeks. I imagined her gasping in the mirror and hurriedly wiping it off, like she did the last morning I saw her.

Ksenia wore a beautiful long-sleeved lace black dress and I knew this was how I was going to remember her, the last memory I would have stored. She held her breath when I hugged her. A toothy American woman was filling Dixie cups with Koliva. A gaggle of stewardesses sat demurely in the third row, only identifiable by their perfect makeup and neat chignons. Black and sleek, arms like the necks of geese. A redhead named Martin who I had never seen before was touching paper icons to Mila's body and passing them around. A custom reserved for bishops, in the event that they become ordained in the future. A beautiful mistake. I took three of the icons for my wallet.

I recognized Zina's puffy hair, sunglasses, kerchief, and cleavage, the only way she would leave the house. She stood alone in a black trench coat, scanning the pews, a television mourner.

"Let's get out of here." I whispered and hooked her arm.

We walked through the neighboring streets, big houses with deep green front yards and long driveways. The type of neighborhood with little free libraries full of trendy novels and foreign policy tomes. A squirrel stuffed its face sitting on an engraved bench. It shrieked as we sat down. Zina took off her scarf and glasses. Her forehead was sweating and she looked afraid, rodent-like, flinching at every passing car and dog walker.

"I haven't seen so many people at once in almost 6 years." She started. "I used to be married. We lived in New York, not too far from Washington Square. Have you been to New York?"

"Only to the airport. When I moved here. But I've seen Seinfeld. And Sex and the City."

"Isaac and I lived on 4th Ave. We had a big Jewish wedding, all four grandmas, endless wine, an ad in the paper, everything *right*." She took a water bottle full of white wine from her purse and took a big sip. She licked her teeth before continuing. "Isaac started to drink more, work less, gain weight, pay Filipinas for sex, skid marks everywhere..."

"What's a skid mark?"

She waved her hand and laughed. "He became an ogre, basically. But one that was constantly telling me that I was a fat, hairy hag who stole his youth and ruined his life. Meanwhile, he never wanted kids, he never wanted me, his best man told me that Isaac married the first JAP to give him the time of day."
   "Who divorced who?"

"Whom."

I dug my nail into my palm.

"I went to my dad's firm and drafted a settlement. It was a bold proposal, honestly, asking for a lot of alimony, but the Ischild letterhead has some sway. I figured, he stole my 20s. I can't put a price on that."

I thought of Mila changing the channel from Lifetime in a fury. I wished she was sitting at my feet.

"How much money?"

She gulped more wine. "Enough for Isaac to tell me he'd only sign off on it if I took off all of my clothes, all of my jewelry, all of my makeup, and walked down three blocks of 5th Avenue at 11 AM, completely naked." Another sip. "And I did it. In nothing but flip flops."

"No shit?" I jumped up and scared a flock of birds picking at the grass nearby. "He lady Godiva'd you?"

"I took the money and left New York. I came back to Maryland, moved less than a mile from my Hebrew school."

"Did anyone film you?"

"Of course. They were vicious. They called me a mental hospital escapee, a homeless woman, a lost prostitute. My family, my friends, they get me work sometimes, they send girls to me, girls who need help. They think if I spend time around someone worse off, I'll wake up, I'll start being a person again. But it never lasts."

"Why do you live in that apartment? Why didn't you buy a house?"

"A house? I can't even maintain my leg hair."

"If I had money, I'd buy land and guns. Some place with a porch and no neighbors. Walk around naked in my yard."

"I've had enough of that."

I grabbed the Deer Park bottle of white wine. A man walked by with two small dogs, too fat for their short legs. He waved at us. We waved back. Zina pulled out a velvet box and set it on my thigh.

"You proposing to me?"

She smirked. "Open it."

Two gold screw back earrings with teardrop opals. Their orange hearts flickered in the sun.

"My uncle never had the conscience to take them. He mailed them to me a week after meeting her. I never remembered to dig them out of my dresser and give them back to Mila. I thought there would be another time, a better time, her wedding, her child's baptism. Something."

A champagne cat sat in the driveway of the house across the street. No collar. It watched us with its paws carefully tucked under its stomach. I held her until my shoulders grew sore.

"I've been asleep." She cried into my unwashed hair. "I never thought I could outlive her."

*

I chewed around my manicure swiping through five different dating apps in a sports bar on the top floor of Pentagon City Mall. I'd decided to look for him. I got a wave of paranoia as an ad for JDate played on three TVs at once. I called Zina from the bathroom.

"They have to put their phones in lockers after going through security. He'll only have it on the commute there and back. Forget it. Enjoy your night. Flirt with someone."

"We have to find out where he lives. Are you sure you don't know him? Is there a database?"

"Of Jews? I could check my yearbooks. Don't get your hopes up, though. There are more Cohns in here than a Baskin-Robbins."

I heard her breathing heavily, looking through a bookshelf. I wanted to give up and go back to the hotel and watch cop shows with a bottle of wine between my knees.

"I could befriend someone who works in the food court and get *them* to poison him. Hang around the metro, looking for Taco Bell uniforms."

"Fast food employees take the bus."

She was right about that. For an agoraphobic, Zina knew plenty about human nature from hours of smoking on her balcony. I sprayed myself with Mila's Givenchy, changed into her blue uniform, and started walking to the bus station.

Hilde was six feet tall with mean pink palms that snatched Carden's chestnut braids out of his hands before haggling over the price. Her tendinous catcher's mitts stroked the hair with a vigor that made him want to accept any price and leave.

He pictured the way those hands grabbed Carden's ponytail last week, stroking it with a greedy thumb as she passed by in the apartment corridors.

"Is the hair being well maintained?" she asked, wrapping her ponytail around her fist, pulling Carden's head at a painful angle. She froze, waiting to be freed. Jem spoke up.

"I brush her hair every night before bed."

Hilde dropped the ponytail and grimaced. "Look at all this damage. I can tell it's been brushed by a rough male hand. I was generous last time— I didn't penalize you for the six inches of split ends. You need to eat more meat. Come to my restaurant."

"Promise me you'll never eat there. She's trying to find a loophole, a way to not pay us. I don't grow my hair out all year for a discount on pork pies," Carden whispered after Hilde's door locked.

"Chicken."

"Smelled like pork yesterday."

She tied a silk scarf over her long, messy hair and cried herself to sleep that night.

Carden always went through a period of mourning the days after the haircuts. She'd cover the mirrors and stay in bed all day. Their apartment felt much smaller those weeks.

"You look so beautiful. Like a girl in a French new wave movie, or a gymnast."

"When I catch my reflection, I think I'm 12 years old again. Did you bring the tape?"

A quiet knock. The little girl next door coming over to play with their cat, a pure white kitten with a little orange smudge on her chest, a bleeding heart. They called her Dolores. Sophie is gentle with her, but eats all her food.

"What happened to your hair?" Sophie asked, munching on kibble.
   "I sold it to Hilde so she can make wigs for people who get to eat every day."
   "You look like a boy."
   "You look like your grandpa."
   "He's bald."

They caught Sophie's grandfather, Arne, putting his trash into their recycling last week. The five seconds that Carden went back inside for her coat, he'd snuck in his yogurt containers and glass bottles. Carden set them all on the ground and pounded on his door. He pretended to not be home and the hallway was full of trash for three days until Jem picked it up. Trash costs $2 a pound to collect. The dumpster weighs each load and doesn't open up until it gets paid.

"Go to sleep, Sophie, I'm in a bad mood today. Jem, did you bring home some tape?"
   "Your nice got cut off with your hair. I'm never cutting mine."
   "Bye," Carden curled up deeper in the sleeping bag. "See you tomor-row."
   "Tomorrow's Friday."
   "She'll try us anyways."

Jem and Carden didn't eat on Fridays. They melted packing tape that Jem stole from the hardware store and huffed the glue until they felt lightheaded bliss for three hours. They'd listen to music and dance and try not to think about food. Their shoulderblades and ribcages formed dunes, wind-worked deserts that bruised against each other, the warp and weft of three hungry years.

*

"Can you read?" Sophie asked, brushing Dolores.
   "Not so well. Not as good as Jem. He's read tons of books."
   "My grandpa can read any word you show him. He reads the news-paper every day."

"Where does he get it?"
"He buys it with his coffee."
"And he doesn't feed you?"
"He says you will. Or Hilde."

"I don't want her coming over anymore." Carden whispered. "We can't let him take advantage of us like that."

She had some kind of hair mask slathered over her scalp. It smelled like honey, garlic, and creosote. Her hair had been falling out again.

"She's just a little girl. Look how hungry she is, eating Dolores' food hand over fist…"
"Let Hilde feed her."

*

A fourth body was found. Part of one. A tattooed leg was found under the chain link fence around the tow lot. A stray dog had tried to drag it under and they both got stuck. A cop had to free them with wire cutters. Sophie was throwing up in a bucket in the hallway. Jem hadn't seen her for days.

"Looks like Hilde's food isn't going down too well for her."
"Are you trying to make me feel guilty?"
"Just saying."
"Tell her she can come with us to the roof when she feels better."

*

"Grandpa says I'm still too sick to go alone. He has to come with us."
"That's fine," Carden pet her head, hiding her disappointment. "Hurry up, we'll catch the sunset."

Jem carried a pile of broken-down cardboard boxes under his arm. Sophie carried a tin of paint markers and the cat.

"Why does Dolores need a leash? She doesn't like it," Sophie whined, scratching the cat's white chin under the fraying nylon webbing.

"Have you ever seen a stray cat around here? If she escapes, Hilde will make her into a meat pie."

Arne twitched at the mention of her name. He hung back a few feet behind Carden, fiddling with his phone.

They settled on the roof of the library, the building with the most impressive Western view. Sophie and Carden drew hearts around their names on the concrete. C+J+S+D+A.

"Take a nice picture of the girls, with the whole vista, from that other roof." Arne suggested, passing Jem his camera. "How many pictures of Carden do you even have?"
 "Not many, none with her short hair. She gets shy."
 "I like the cut. She looks French, a little Anna Karina."
 "That's exactly what I said."

They watched Jem cross the courtyard to the Math building and crawl up to the roof in his bright green jacket, the camera slung across his chest.

"I got him that for his birthday. It fits him so perfect. And I can see him biking home from work half a mile away."

He stepped backwards, one eye in the lens, his curls falling over the camera. He waved his left hand and held up three fingers, counting down. Three navy blue men climbed up the ladder behind him and grabbed that left arm, folding it behind his back. Arne's camera cracked against the concrete roof.

"Don't lose Dolores!" Carden yelled as she climbed down from the roof.
 She ran through the courtyard to the cop cars parked around the other building. The crowd of Community Witnesses was on the other side of it. She heard their megaphones and applause before she saw them. She joined the front row, where a group of Expert Witnesses convened in a circle.

A blonde man with a tanned forehead and receding hairline congratulated Carden with a job well done. He made his rounds, squeezing shoulders and slapping backs with his good arm. The other was in a sling. He seemed to have some kind of authority. She stayed to eavesdrop on the Witnesses, trying to understand how Jem was accused.

"His coworker said he carried around a bag of his victims' hair in his backpack. Sick fuck." A round woman pulled her sweater tighter. Her Expert Witness badge sat parallel to the ground atop her huge chest.
　"Untrackable. The guy used a pager from the late 80's."
　"What's with serial killers and old tech?"

A man with long blonde dreads banged a djembe and pumped the crowd of Witnesses into a frenzy. They stomped and clapped and howled. The cops had long guns in their arms and short ones on their hips. She barely saw Jem's green jacket in the tinted backseat as they drove into town.

Sophie was waiting in the landing between their apartments.
　"Can you feed Dolores? I'm hungry."
　Carden took Dolores off her leash and went inside without a word. She flicked two fingers at Sophie. *Shoo.*

The next day she put on her warmest clothes, sturdiest shoes, and walked into town to look for a new job. She'd been a Watcher for almost a year; watching her screen for ten hours a day proctoring tests, loss prevention, surveilling warehouses. She'd connect to various CCTV around the city and press a button every time she caught a cheater or a thief or a slacker.

The main road through campus was built for a time when everyone drove their own cars. The big metal gate was rusted and left ajar all day and night. The amphitheater was full of trash, as was every creek, pond, and valley. Walmart had a deal with local developers, an effective system for herding the homeless. They dumped truckloads of tents, camping stoves, and sleeping bags into the middle of a clearing and waited for word to spread. One of these was right on the outskirts of campus. She'd seen pictures and movies of homeless camps of the past, they never quite looked realistic. How did they afford all that spray paint?

The stained glass window of an exchurch was covered with a big nylon flag: a gold star in the center of an eyeball. The same symbol Expert Witnesses wore on their badges. She went inside.

The basement was full of people holding paper plates and white cups. A long table parallel to the windows was laden with cookies, coffee, croissants, sliced bread, peanut butter, jelly and all kinds of food.

She recognized some of the people from Jem's arrest, jumping around in the front row. The man in a sling was in a wheelchair today, a megaphone hanging off the back handle.

"Donovan," he introduced himself, wheeling towards Carden. "Are you new?"

"Yeah, I was at the last arrest."

"I thought you looked familiar. That was a good one! Major catch. Take a plate."

Carden thought about stealing the jar of peanut butter. It would be enough calories for two weeks; she could even start eating on Fridays. She thought about cameras and put it back down after spreading a generous amount on her bread.

"Did you get paid last time?"

"Uh, no, it was pretty busy. I must have slipped through the cracks."

"Yeah, big turnout yesterday. I'll get you a flier with the payment breakdown."

> Second row: $20
> Front row: $60
> Level 3 injury: $100
> Level 2 injury: $200
> Level 1 injury: $900

"What's a level 1 injury?" she asked.

"Getting shot, burned, or otherwise disabled."

"Is that what happened to you?"

Donovan winked and wheeled himself over to the plate of cookies. His candor about money was refreshing. Carden kept eating peanut butter. She felt full and relieved and started to feel hope for herself and Jem.

*

Sophie threw her door open like she'd been waiting for Carden through the peephole.

"Can I come play with Dolores?" she screeched. "I've been waiting all day. Why weren't you home today?"

Carden peered into the apartment above Sophie's head. Arne was at the table reading a book with a cup of coffee. He had a new toupee, a suspiciously chestnut piece that clashed with his gray pattern balding.

"I've been busy." Carden raised her voice. "My boyfriend, whose job allowed us to live in this apartment, was falsely arrested yesterday."

Arne slowly lifted the newspaper to obscure his face.

"Nice toupee. Did you get that from Hilde?"

"She brought it this morning." Sophie interrupted. "In a pretty bag."

Arne stood up and pulled Sophie from the door. "No cats today."

*

"Carden!" Donovan called, limping over on a pair of crutches. "Here's the $20 from last time, and a little extra, as a welcome."

"How do I use this?" Carden asked, looking at the plastic card. It carried the same insignia as the badges.

"Just tap it like a regular card. Think of it as a gift card you can use anywhere. Anywhere legal, that is. If you try to buy anything weird, it'll stop working, you'll get fired, and you won't be able to access your balance."

"Define weird."

"Guns, livestock, crypto, and any ingredients you'd use to make bombs and meth."

"I don't even—"

"Don't worry, there's no rule against buying peanut butter. I saw you housing it last time, ordered some more. Forgot to ask, crunchy or creamy?"

"Both. Creamy is good on celery and sandwiches, crunchy is good by itself."

"She's flexible. Easygoing. A team player. Glad to have you, Carden." Donovan limped over to a newcomer, identifiable by his lack of CW sticker. Donovan said she'd get promoted from a sticker to a badge in no time.

*

Sleeping in the apartment without Jem's ambient snoring was next to impossible. Carden stuffed tissue in her ears to block out the moan of the furnace, the Chinese water torture drip of the broken gutters, the sneaky whistle of wind slipping through poorly insulated windows. He was the orange heart of the opal, the sun in the sky, the slice of lemon in the water glass. In his absence, she began to hear, see, notice, and sense everything.

A quiet knock at a strange time. 5 AM. Carden wiggled out of her sleeping bag and slowly approached the peephole. Sophie's face filled the glass. Another knock, this time louder. Carden put her ear up to the door. The knock was coming from above her head. Someone much taller than Sophie wanted in.

She stepped back slowly, grateful for the thick metal fire doors that had been guarding these dormitories since it was full of students eighty years ago. She crawled back into her sleeping bag and caught herself talking to someone, someone who wasn't Jem, but loved her just as much. Someone she'd never seen, never met, but heard of. Someone who lived above the basement she worked in now, the man upstairs. She'd heard people pray before but never up close, never anyone her age, never anyone she knew personally.

*

Carden caught up to Donovan as they piled into vans, ready to be transported to the day's arrest.

"We're busting up an illegal day care today. Get ready for some baby-ops."

"Great, I look good in pastels."

"There she goes with that great attitude."

"So Donovan, I wanted to ask, how do you guys get your intel?"

"The Community Witness network is huge. We have opportunities for people to Witness without even getting off their couches. They can call or text with tips on suspicious characters and unsavory activity. If their tips are corroborated by another CW member, both of them get paid. It's like a referral program."

"And the cops check up on their leads?"

"If they have time, yeah. But most of the time, if there's fire, there's smoke."

"What if someone calls in false information, and gets someone else to collude with them?"

"That's illegal."

"But it must happen, no?"

"Anything's possible," Donovan clicked with his cheek. "It's almost go time. Did you want to look through the prop bag?"

He handed her a bag of slings, eyepatches, gauze, glaucoma glasses, finger splints, and epilepsy helmets. She chose the glasses.

Carden took a long, hot shower after getting home from the arrest. The sound of babies crying and children panicking and young women trying to placate kids and cops and Witnesses knotted her shoulders. She curled up on the tiles and cried to God again.

*

"Don't you miss Jem? He was so nice to you. Nicer than me."

"Grandpa said Jem is fake nice. *Duplicitous.*"

"That's a big word. He been teaching you how to read?"

"Yeah, with a dictionary. We have lots of them."

"Can you bring me one? I'll only borrow it for one day. I have to write Jem a letter."

"He'll be mad at me."

"He won't find out."

There was no chance more than one of the prison guards had anything above a grade school vocabulary, if that. She wrote a letter using words only Jem would know interspersed with simple expressions of love. "Stay buoyant! Love, Carden" she ended it, with a little drawing of a green bottle floating in the ocean. She licked the envelope and walked to work. "What if I found the person dumping bodies in the lake?"

"We already did, last week."

"The broadcast said there was another body found last night. Why are you so certain you caught the right guy?"

"Because we have an airtight intel network, Carden. Almost eleven years of polishing up this system."

"An *airtight network*? Of random volunteers? Of hungry, broke, struggling people with no short term memory?"

"Alright, where's that Card I know and like?"

"I think I know what's happening to those bodies. Let's talk over lunch. Do you like soul food?"

Hilde raised an eyebrow at them from behind the counter. She put one finger up and two meat pies slid into the brick oven on a paddle. Donovan pulled a chair out for Carden before sitting down. It took him a while— he was back in his wheelchair today.

"What's with the props?"

"It reminds people of our heroism and sacrifice."

"*Heroism.* You a reader?"

"I get the paper every day."

Hilde brought two plastic cups of water to their table, giving Donovan a slight bow. "Thank you for your heroism and sacrifice."

"See?" he winked, taking a big sip of his water. Carden kept her hands in her lap.

"I'm taking mine home in a box, I'm not so hungry."

"Really? You suggested this place. Good pork, very tender."

"It's chicken, allegedly."

"Nah, there ain't no way. This is the other white meat. Well, this chunk has a bit of a navy blue tinge…"

Carden took her cup and meat pie to the police station. Donovan wheeled ahead of her, holding each door open for her. He was always at his most chivalrous sitting down.

"Let me do most of the talking, okay? I deal with cops all the time." He rolled to a policeman's desk with the cup in a plastic bag.

"I'd like this tested for prints. Express."

"Is this person a suspect in any crime?"

"Yes, the mur—"

"We have reason to believe the woman who owns this restaurant has not been paying property taxes. We believe she may be guilty of multiple serious financial crimes including tax evasion and failure to update her quarterly mercantile permits."

"*Mercantile?*" she whispered.

Donovan winked and shrugged.

"And this, well this is just simply upsetting. You see, this woman has a Kosher Pareve sticker on her window, but there is no way she is being honest about the ingredients of her meat pies. This has to be pork. And rancid pork, at that. Look at this blue spot!"

"Thanks for coming in, Donovan. We'll have your answers by Friday."

"Shalom."

*

The Community Witnesses buzzed around town with excitement and fear. Donovan pulled an eyepatch out of his pocket and rolled up to the restaurant.

"Big catch today," he nodded at another man wearing a badge. "Tell Ben to get closer to the cameras."

"Can you believe it? She was feeding us stray cats, pigeons, rats, and *homeless* women. Someone found part of a tattoo in their meat pie."

"Disgusting." Another woman whispered. "They'd kill her if she did that back in Haiti."

"She? They ran her prints and found out her real name is Louis Cadet, a human trafficker that escaped from a Miami prison. She put on heels and a wig and started a new life up here."

"Carden, front row today?" Donovan tweaked the new badge pinned below her collarbone.

"She's my neighbor. Maybe I'll hang back."

"It's actually more effective if the criminals recognize their Community Witnesses. Humiliation before familiars is a useful accountability tool."

"I'll just film today."

She signed out a camcorder from the news van parked surreptitiously behind the hardware store. She recognized one of Jem's coworkers on a cigarette break, and wondered how he could afford them. She waved to him and he tucked his chin down, heading back inside without finishing his smoke. She took the half ashed cigarette off the sidewalk and enjoyed two greedy drags.

Carden climbed up the roof of the building across the street. It was too high to catch the arrest; you could barely see Donovan in his wheelchair. She flashed her Expert Witness badge to a security guard who let her into an empty office with a perfect view of the restaurant. She angled the camcorder towards the awning of Carrefour, slowly panning across the block, across the Community Witnesses who were milling around, pretending to be ice cream lickers and athleisure shoppers and soul food eaters. A piercing siren erupted in the left half of Carden's head. She pulled her earbud out until it stopped. Donovan had tripped the silent alarm that alerted cops and Community Witnesses to get in formation. There were twice as many Witnesses as when Jem was arrested on the roof. They linked arms in a semicircle, the two men on the edges pressing tightly against the storefront of the restaurant. The chain only broke to allow six policemen into Carrefour. Carden hit record.

Hilde ran out of the restaurant, past the cops, wielding a long wooden SKS. She fired into the front row of Witnesses, unloading three rounds into Donovan's chest. Another Witness pulled him away and Hilde used the gap between them to run. Her long chestnut wig fell to the ground. A second row Witness snatched it and started to cheer as the cops tackled her to the ground. Carden winced as she watched her hair get torn apart by the eager crowd. She kept the camcorder steady until the first police car pulled away.

Donovan was being loaded into a stretcher. He waved her into the ambulance and showed her the bruising on his chest.

"Vintage Kevlar, baby. I'm totally fine. Just winded. And I just made 900 bucks."

"We should celebrate when you get out."

"Hell yeah. We can get soul food again." He winked and took a deep, painful breath. "I'm recommending you for a promotion."

"No thanks, I might just go back to my old job once they let Jem out of prison."

"If you weren't so attached to that cheap old pager system, you'd know he's already out. I invited him to be in the front row today. Would've been a powerful photo op, no?"

"I'm glad he didn't show. He doesn't own any vintage Kevlar."

"If you quit tomorrow, I'll miss you. But even if you don't, you won't have to sell your hair this year."

Carden bought a heavy bag of groceries and walked back home. The sunset glowed orange and pink all over campus and a green sleeve waved at her through the window of her bedroom.

The Reagan-Blair Manifesto

A COP SCOLDED me back into my room as I tried to walk my bike down the hallway of my dorm. I keep going, trying to pin their caution tape back up before it catches on my handlebars again. I tell the policemen I'm going to group therapy for sexual assault victims in the Social Sciences building and it sounds like a lie but they ease up.

Reagan was early for therapy too, waiting cross-legged on a coffee table. She doesn't trust public upholstery. "Scabies, bedbugs, lice, and ringworm are like herpes," she tells me. "Even when they're gone you'll feel the itch. This furniture is cursed. Built by slaves of the Commonwealth, cheap prison labor contracted out by VCE. 20 cents an hour. Hexed with the blood, sweat, and tears of murderers, rapists, and speeders who went 15 over on 66 on the 31st of the month."

"Quota."

I looked up at the flickering fluorescent lights and tried to picture my rapist sanding wood in an assembly line. It didn't play. My phone was about to die and I reached for the charging station when Reagan stopped me.

"They can get all your data that way. Do you know what a USB is, Blair?"

"They?"

She waved her hand around the lobby. The Social Sciences building was quiet, save for a group of international students in ironed clothes and blindwhite sneakers, talking and laughing on the couch behind me.

"Koreans?"

"Anyone. They could drain your bank account in ten minutes."

"Can't tap a dry well. Anyway, I need to check the news. Did you hear about the sophomore who killed himself last night? He lived on my

84

floor."

"Aaron Ross. Word's been going around. That was *your* dorm? Did you hear the gunshot?"

"No— I heard he hung himself? But it's all blocked off. Curtains and caution tape."

"Did you know him well?"

"Not really, to be honest. More of a business relationship."

"Weed?"

"Adderall."

"I never met him. I saw him around the student union though, always with that commie, Tammy Wu."

"I don't think she's a real commie, I think she just calls everyone comrade because it's provocative, yet gender neutral. Or some kind of military fetish. But I could be wrong, she had a bunch of flags in her room— and not one hammer and sickle. They gave me a weird vibe though. What girl puts flags up?"

"When were you in her room?" Reagan looked annoyed, almost jealous.

I leaned in close enough to smell the lemon oil that binds her single dreadlock that she's always playing with, twisted from the center of her nape, thin enough to hide in a blonde chignon when she goes to work.

"Between you and me, Aaron had some outstanding debts. I paid him two days ago and he didn't come through."

"The cops have probably long seized all his drugs and cash."

"Not quite. Aaron's room is right next to the RA's suite. A few months ago, he started getting paranoid and keeping everything at Tammy's. She lives off campus in one of the co-op houses. I went there yesterday, to see if I could settle things. Nobody was home, so I went into her room."

"And she had some flags? So does every college kid. What do you expect, Bruegel?"

"Her room was decorated with normal stuff, like candles and fairy lights, but also military portraits and still-creased flags I didn't recognize. Red and black, black and yellow. A dragon in a circle, maybe. The room reeked of polyester and packing materials, like Saran wrap had been peeled off everything moments before I came in."

"Did you find what you were looking for?"

I took Reagan's hand and put it inside my backpack. She squeezed around and gasped at a shrink-wrapped bag of little blue footballs.

"What is that, a half pound?" Reagan can guess any weight, volume, and distance with surprising accuracy. Probably from years of weighing groceries at Whole Foods and parallel parking her minivan. "Shrink wrap— that's odd. That's very…involved."

"It's Xanax. Footballs, not bars. Harder to flip, but less likely to be fake. I also took a bottle of Vyvanse and a zip. I gave up on finding cash. A wave of paranoia told me to get the fuck out of Tammy Wu's bedroom."

"At least you got something before finals."

"There was something odd about her place. Neither a razor in her shower nor a lid on her bathroom trash can."

"Some Asians really are that hairless."

"Then where does she throw her tampons?"

"Maybe she uses Diva cups."

"Maybe she has an IUD."

"Maybe it's Maybelline."

"Maybe she has her tubes tied."

"I can see that for her, the activist type."

"A young, beautiful, fertile, yet unimpregnable Ayn Rand heroine."

Reagan curled her top lip. "She's not that pretty. But I can't believe you didn't invite me to break into Red Guard Barbie's bedroom with you."

"It was impulsive."

"How much speed have you been taking?"

"There's Rachel. Let's go upstairs."

Our group therapist was waiting for the elevator to the 4th floor. Rachel Eisenberg was a middle aged brunette with tight curls that always looked wet. We waited behind her but she didn't acknowledge us until we were inside the elevator. The lengths she went to adhere to the rule that we weren't supposed to approach each other outside of therapy was almost comical. When I ran into her last week she didn't even hold the door for me. I think she wished she could kick us out for becoming friends outside of group. She had lots of other rules, so many that they became a tight grid. No interactions outside of group, no descriptions of sexual assault, no identifying details about our rapists, no discussions of self harm, eating disorders, substance abuse, or suicidal thoughts. Rachel enforced her rules with a small hand bell that she used as a gavel. She rang it every time someone crossed the double yellow lines. I was the first one to lose the conch today.

"Blair, I need to cut you off. This is a gentle reminder to everyone else that they need to be mindful not to share any details that could trigger your peers. We're not here to discuss what happened, we're here to share how we've been *coping*. Coping mechanisms can be healthy, or they can be maladaptive. You can share any insights about cop-"

"Anything except cutting and k-holes. Right." Reagan waved away her turn to share. She rested her head on her fist and kept chewing her lip while the rest of us watercolored mood maps. She walked me back to my dorm.

"Sometimes group feels like Sunday school. Or when you go to confession and you can't tell the priest your real sins so you make a few up, wasting everyone's time." I hadn't been to church in three years. I wondered if Reagan ever has. Religion seemed to be a sore spot for her. She twisted her dread around her finger, pausing before she answered.

"Have you noticed that everything in therapy is designed so that we don't know a single thing about each other? We can't say anything about who, what, where, or when we were raped. We can't even say how old we were. We can't be honest about how we've dealt with it. We can't even acknowledge each other outside of that one little conference room. We could have all been attacked by the same guy and we'd never know. There could be serial rapists on campus that they're unwittingly protecting."

We got silent for a moment. The descending dusk made me tense and vigilant. I noticed she was scanning too.

"A few months ago, on New Year's, I overdid it at a party and my friend asked her boyfriend to give me a ride home. I was tired and wasted and cold and didn't think anything of it. I knew him. Besides, he's an EMT, he's good at driving drunk. But I never got home. I woke up before sunrise, shivering and choking on a condom. You know the big flower bed that spells out G-C-U in petunias, the one you pass as you pull into campus drive? I was in the middle of the C."

"Mine happened outside, too. A year ago I was leaving an AA meeting in that white church near the bike trail, off Braddock. There was this guy in the meeting, Sandy, who kept trying to get my number so he could be my sponsor. I got bad vibes and ignored him. He followed me to my car, knocked the keys out of my hand, and dragged me into the woods behind the parking lot. When I found my phone and called the cops, he was already long gone. The cops searched my bag and arrested me for half a joint. I spent a night in jail and I'm still on probation. Speak of the devil—"

She pointed to the cop parked on the sidewalk in front of my dorm, talking to my RA who hadn't changed out of her PJ's today. She was holding two phones in one hand and kept pulling her bike shorts down with the other. She pointed at me and got his attention.

"Our floor is blocked off tonight. Resident Life should have emailed you a few hours ago. You were supposed to make other arrangements." She looked apologetic. I still resented her.

"My phone died."

"Stay at my place tonight," Reagan tugged on my sleeve.

Reagan's van is like a mullet: superclean in the front, disaster in the back. Two big water jugs rested on a nest of board game pieces, tarot cards, single gloves, bandaid wrappers, tea-stained jars, tie-dyed bandanas, salt crystal deodorant, and the Edward Cayce rosewater spray. She rented a basement from two grad students who lived 20 minutes from campus in a quiet neighborhood with a fake lake.

"How do you know which house is yours?" I asked, not realizing how rude my question sounded before it left my mouth.
  "Ticky tacky central, I know. I drive right by it sometimes when my roommate isn't home. His purple Chevy Malibu stands out in the driveway."
  "That one stands out, too." I pointed to the DHS crest painted on a white SUV. Reagan shivered behind the wheel. I tucked my backpack under my knees.

We inventoried the loot from Tammy's on the carpet under the glow of the TV. Some of it was sampled in the process.

"I almost forgot about this." I slid Aaron's journal across the carpet, a green leather Moleskin with GCU embossed in gold. "This was pushed to the back of the drawer with the Xanax. Aaron's ledger. I always thought it was clunky of him to jot our transactions down in a notebook. And a good way to get caught. I couldn't leave it there for the cops to find."

"You're so nosy," Reagan gasped. "I can't wait to read this." She flipped through the pages of numbers, initials, symbols, profits, and debts. "Does a red triangle mean Adderall? Is this you, B.A.?" she tsked at me, shaking her head. "You kept him in business til the very end."

"Could be other customers, he had the decency to only use initials. But besides, he lived three doors down the hall from me. It was convenient. Why would I go to anyone else?"

"Either he was ripping you off, or you're a real guzzler. A fiend."

"So are you. Get a ziploc from the kitchen."

I filled it up for her like Halloween, like that house with the full candy bars and something to prove. She flipped onto her stomach, slowly reading through Aaron's journal, looking up at me from time to time.

"Have you read this, Blair?" She twisted her dread and chewed the inside of her lip with a little too much heart. It's easy to rile her up.

"I flipped through it earlier, mostly just to see if and how much I was incriminated."

She took a bobby pin out of her hair and used it as a bookmark.

"Start here, early March. It's boring before that, online poker debts and other transactions, like selling his Xbox on February 23rd, owing Tammy $48 for dinner on February 27th. Imagine owing your girlfriend money."

"Who'd he sell the Xbox to? I saw one in her bedroom."

"He sold it to a 'T.W.' Blair, do you remember when she had those little ads up? She was posting these little fliers: *My house got broken into, looking for a new TV and gaming console. Thank you, comrades!*"

"My eyes glaze over when I see the co-op pinboard. It's just ads for ukulele lessons and Hare Krishna propaganda pinned over the stolen bike memorial wall. I think I saw it online, though."

"I was wondering how they met. He doesn't seem like someone who hangs out at the co-op."

"You think she lured him to her house by buying a Xbox off him?"

"It's the perfect ploy. Think about it— how much does an Xbox cost?"

"No idea."

"Exactly. Girls don't know that shit. He emails Tammy saying he has one for a *bargain* of $300, hoping she doesn't haggle down. This puts him into a *category*. It lowers his ESG. He ripped a woman off. An *Asian* woman. A friendly, gainfully employed woman who has recently experienced the tragedy of having her home broken into. Her safe space— violated.

The Xbox is heavy, he'll have to deliver it himself. Into her bedroom. Tammy knows this, and she's ready, answering the door in little dolphin shorts and a ribbed tank, maybe something with the om or ying yang symbol to make her seem like a hippy and put free love on his mind. *'Right there, on the floor, wow I could never lift that by myself. Do you want a drink? Are you on Discord? Are you on any SSRIs?'* Meanwhile, Aaron's not listening to her but he's still somehow answering all her questions in the affirmative. You know why men are so retarded when they're horny? Listen to this."

Reagan straddled me on the couch with her palms so tight against my ears it created an uncomfortable suction. I heard a wind tunnel, frequencies, shifting liquids, a crackling in my neck.

"I hear the ocean."

"You hear blood leaving your head and saliva rushing in to replace it. Red and white, black and white, yin yang." Reagan jumped back onto the floor and paced into the kitchen. "So he goes over there. And Tammy fucks him without trying because there is nothing better for a man than a fuck he didn't prepare for. For a woman, nothing's worse, you didn't have time to shave or bathe or make sure you aren't ovulating. Are you on birth control?"

"No, you?"

"Fuck no. Hysteria and infertility are extremely profitable for the elites. Open your bank app right now. You'll see that you spend more money in the last six days of your luteal phase than you do all month."

"There is no way I'm looking at my bank account right now."

"You'll see I'm right."

"I have a progesterone prescription, but I'm lazy. I never remember to pick it up. I sold my last month of it to this girl at a frat party. I told her it was molly."

"A perfect crime. When it doesn't work, you can just blame it on her Prozac."

"Safe bet. It's really a rite of passage, come to college and blunt the pain of your unattainable expectations with prescription drugs…but what did Tammy want with Aaron?"

"Chaos. Ever since the Columbine prototype was released in 1995, schools have been churning out school shooters like tagliatelle. Tag, you're it. Tagged like a dolphin. Red wax on a roach's back. A lone wolf, a scapegoat. The government creates hundreds of these men and keeps them in cryostorage for years. They're bred like goldfish and they only use a handful. All over the country we have guys fermenting in dorms and basements and bedrooms decked out with triple monitors and gaming systems and books they hoped that would change their lives when they caught themselves in a rare, sober moment, after their caffeine hit but before the anxiety set in, the moment where they pause and feel something before reaching for their bong to push that thought away. Guys who spend every waking moment online and start to feel guilty for all of it. Victimized by all of it. Powerless to any little bit of it except the nuclear option. Online advertising algorithms can sense that my roommate is a depressed woman in her early 30's who desperately wants her boyfriend to propose so she can have a reason to reconnect with all of her friends who she ghosted two years ago because she was afraid of them seeing her weight gain. Of course that same algorithm can easily pinpoint Aaron as a young, lonely, drug-dealing, third-generation descendant of Holocaust survivors who inherited a weak constitution and inherent distrust of the establishment."

"You got all this from Aaron's journal?"

"I tended bar in a hotel near Aurora last summer. It's where people stay when they're just in Denver for the airport, if you know what I mean. And remember that night in jail? I learned a lot from those ladies. Now read this."

I didn't know Aaron was left handed. His boy handwriting was legible, but smudged over with a smog of blue ink.

3/02/18
Dragon symbol, yellow on black, "*we own the night.*" Proba-

bly anime. Find out.

3/15/18
J Cole at the Patriot Center

3/18/18
VA Tech shooter = westfield alum

4/19/18
Look up:
MK Ultra
Artichoke
Bluebird
Collins-Armirgo project.
Gladio
Danny Casolero and the octopus
Delgado and the bull
Estabrooks/Delgado/Verdier

4/24/18
Delgado could start and stop a charging bull with a micro chip.
Danny turns 6 on Friday. Don't forget to buy him a birthday present (Remote control Hot Wheels)

4/30/18
Ate meat in front of Tammy yesterday. She's mad.
Only drink alone from now on.

5/3/18
Moonies
Manson Family
Blacksburg

Reagan erased her roommates' white board and tore it off the kitchen wall. She ran out of writing space and gave up on it, tucking it under the couch. She opened a fresh page in Aaron's journal.

5/19/18
Trauma sends you back into the cocoon by inflicting a dissociative, submissive, and inward state.

Evangelical organizations swoop in on the victim's families after highly publicized tragedies involving guns and bombs. Federally contracted grief counselors are released into schools, setting up shop in empty classrooms armed with tissue boxes and worksheets. For the girls, some fed's menopausal wife in Chicos and a beaded glasses chain. For the guys, an ex football coach with a rap sheet riddled with bad touches and CP, trotted out when he was needed, but kept on a short leash.

Rachel rings her bell whenever someone starts to get into detail about what was done to them. After a while we stop trying to tell anyone about it.

They're trying to program us in group therapy.

"Did I tell you what happened to me the other night?" I asked, painting my toenails to match hers. "I was in the elevator with a full basket of laundry when this blonde man, in some kind of linen safari outfit, pointed to my feet and said, 'aren't those some *suckable little piggies!*' He said it like a joke, but never took his eyes off them. I kinda laughed it off. The next day I was telling my friends about it when this one girl, Kerri, starts freaking out. Apparently a man fitting that description was following her around campus, asking her about her feet and her childhood."

"You *do* have some cute toes. You should've let Crocodile Dundee—"

"That guy tried to break into her apartment last week. She first saw him in Starbucks. He correctly guessed her shoe size and kept asking her how she liked growing up in Blacksburg. He banged on the door for a while, left her a new pair of sandals in size 6 ½, and ran away before the cops came…"

"Blacksburg," Reagan whispered.

She started to draw a table.

    Location + proximity to Westfield High:
    Blacksburg/VA Tech-242 miles
    Blacksburg Mountain-276 miles
    NRO Taj Mahal building-0.9 miles
    Premium Distributors of VA LLC-0.6 miles
    Northrop Grumman-2.8 miles
    Lockheed Martin-7.3 miles

Reagan was biting her cuticles until they bled and I rubbed lotion on them but it didn't stop her. I shouldn't have given her my usual dose of Adderall.

"They're cooking something up in a DARPA lab 7,000 feet under a mountain near Blacksburg. Cooking up something good at the Mac Demarco show. They're putting something in the beer that makes everyone disassociate. No one wakes up until they're 27. It's one big club and we're already in it."

She pulled out a laptop and started typing like she had a vendetta against the keys. I mixed a drink and went to the porch for fresh air and a smoke.

"Why do serial killers and school shooters have first names for a last name? Three last names? Three first names? Who decides that? They all sound like presidents…"
    "We sound like presidents."
    "Reagan Spencer… Blair Adams…you have a point."
    I fell asleep to the sound of the printer spitting pages out on the carpet next to me.

*

The next morning we took the bus back to campus and entered the basketball stadium with Reagan's roommates' IDs ready to be scanned. The jarhead with red hair beeped their barcodes without a second look. He had a square and compass tattooed on his thick forearms. Reagan squeezed my hand to make sure I noticed.

We blended into the stadium of college kids in dark shades of late May athleisure. Half of the crowd was wearing baseball caps and drawstring backpacks like ours. Paper is heavy. The drawstrings dug into my hungover shoulders. Aaron's photo was blown up on a big white poster that a few people had signed. Mostly teachers. A social worker/therapist, you could tell by her glasses chain, was manning a card table with stacks of fliers boasting all the mental health resources available on campus. We stood by while a volunteer took a stack of fliers and started passing them out around the bleachers. He didn't stop to look and realize he'd been handing out our alternative reading.

*

Aaron Ross was a victim of Programming

His subconscious was flooded with subliminal violence and desperation as many hours a day as his eyes stayed open. He was identified, medicated, isolated, and then drawn out with a leash for his big experiment. A monkey in a cage in a warehouse in New Rochelle. The final stage of his programming was completed through his handler Tammy Wu. The only uncertainty left was suicide or homicide: which direction will the rotten tree fall?

> *Say NO to the grief counselors that are sweeping into campus today*
> *They are trained to take advantage of collective tragedy.*
> *They want you isolated, addicted, paranoid, and obedient.*
> *They aim to Program you.*
> *They are here because the iron is hot.*

> *GCU's therapy offerings are a bitter placebo*

They scold and confuse and shush you until you just stop trying to tell the truth. R.E., LCSW, interrupts you with a handbell when you've said the wrong thing. The two notes that begin an SVU episode. Two notes every time you say something honest, before you see a TV woman decomposing on asphalt, and when the stranger you see every week tries to open up. Two notes that paint you into a corner until you choose isolation, overeating, and drugs over honesty, community, and conversation.

> *Bells come in many forms*

The crack of a beer
The flick of a lighter
Every flag you see hanging
Every time Tammy Wu calls you Comrade

How do I know if I am a victim of Programming as well?

Are you alone? Do you allow yourself to be vulnerable around others? Do you sleepwalk? Do you dissociate while driving, biking, or taking public transportation? Do you take prescription drugs? Do you take recreational drugs? Do you sell drugs? Do you make friends online? Have you sought therapy? Have you met with grief, addiction, or relationship counselors? Have you been sexually assaulted?

Are there Programmers at other universities?

There are too many Programmers to count. Some of them don't know who they are Programming for. Some of them don't even know that they are Programmers. Some of them are put on the news to Program us all. Dylan, Eric, James, Adam, and Seung Hui. Elizabeth Holmes was raped at a Stanford frat party before she went out for blood. Both of Mattress Girl's parents are psychiatrists. Her father was a crisis counselor for 9/11 survivors. Apple, meet tree.

Why would they do this to us?

Every woman loves a brute. Every campus loves a Mattress Girl. She makes it look like they aren't in control. No control, no blame. No blame, no shame stopping them from using every weakness of human nature to modify behavior and become architects of society, molding adolescents and young adults into infoslaves.

We waited on the bleachers to watch how people would react once they started reading the manifesto. But they didn't. Once the free cupcakes ran out students started leaving the stadium, crumpling paper into the trash. Reagan started to twist her dread, staring into the overhead lights, trying not to blink. I took her hand and walked her to the student union for breakfast.

The Great Wave Off Kawasaki

My BROTHER constantly needed to *feel good*. Ferric dust chasing a magnet. He stayed up all night sawing cardboard boxes with the bread knife because it caused a pleasant vibration from his fingers up to his arms. He chewed on electrical cables until they frayed and sliced my silk ribbons with kitchen scissors just to hear the whirr. He carved every bar of soap into perfect spheres. He ran water over his fingers for hours and filled the bathtub with dozens of bottles of mom's seltzer because the bubbles carved sounds that bored into his head like insect trails in tree bark. Fireworks on a slow shutter speed. He held my head under the bathwater until I heard it too.

He got suspended for imposing his will upon his wheelchair bound classmate, a big drooling girl who could barely speak. I could see her mother's spine extend, then relax once she stepped into our living room. She stroked the arm of our damask couch and said *yes, I'd love some ginseng tea* and her husband had some questions for my dad about our $20,000 sound system. The four of them twisted in the living room for an hour, avoiding the subject, and no one thanked me for the tea. Then the moms hugged and my dad got a clap on the back and nothing further ever happened to my brother.

When the waitress hands you a chipped mug, you just twist the crack away from your lip. You don't make a fuss. You just give it back to her when you're done. Two hours later, someone else twists that same mug the same way. Every day.

Shame is the only way to catch the attention of the wealthy; it ignites a hot, dry rage inside them. Lose the race, kill the horse. A poor person may live their lives with only brief respites from shame— shame about their cheap clothes, dented car, and tiny apartment, guestless, living in spaces they wouldn't dare reveal to company. But they're used to it. They don't even notice it— how often can you see your own nose, even when you cross your eyes?

One summer our house was being photographed for Architectural Digest. Dad was showing the photographer his built-in bookshelves, leather chair, and oriental carpets. He demonstrated the sloping hutch of his agarwood writing desk, rolling it up and down. My brother loved that sound. He almost broke it, opening and shutting it for hours. Enough for my dad to start locking the den. It was for the better; I couldn't stand to be in that room. I could tell my dad slept in there from the way it smelled. Raising Cain was often on his desk, full of bookmarks.

My brother heard the hutch's warm wooden rumble and ran upstairs. Then I heard the printer in the den start up and my dad yelling for the photographers to leave the room. The printer was spitting out dozens of copies of photos of my brother, wrapped in a rubber band until his skin was blue. You couldn't say it was a finger; he'd kept his open fly in the frame. I crawled behind the desk, pushing it with the side of my body and straining against its weight to form a gap between the wall so I could reach the socket and unplug the printer.

"There's dust all over your clothes," Dad said to me once I crawled back out. "Get changed."

Out to dinner, my brother noticed a chubby woman in a tight velvet dress. He called her over. He started to feel her sleeves and hips and squeezed divots into her skin with his fingers. She laughed and looked around nervously and backed into a waiter and I pried his hands off her and my brother wrapped his arm around my neck and pulled me out of my chair. My mouthful of seltzer burned my nose as I fell backwards. I felt Blue Velvet step on my hair as my brother pulled her into my seat.

The ride home was so quiet I could hear the $1200 of food and wine digesting inside of the four of us.

A week later my dad bought him a motorcycle.

My brother found his soulmate in the Kawasaki, in the vibration that encompassed his body as he rode up and down the highway. He started to disappear. The long showers stopped, along with the flooded bathrooms and soap sculptures. We stopped waking up to piles of shredded paper and cloth, cracked kitchen tiles that he tried to pry out, and chewed up phone chargers. He'd walk upstairs without taking off helmet. We went days without seeing his face.

The tension my brother created was replaced with the tension of losing our scapegoat. My behavior was dissected with an almost superstitious vigor. My brother was a tsunami. The crash of the wave was always preceded by delusory silence. A slingshot. An empty beach drying in the sun, littered with crabs and oysters and flapping fish that would warn you if they could.

*

"I've seen this before. It's not so uncommon— when a heavier gal is riding pillion, we get a tragedy of physics."

"Thank you for explaining that." My mother remained diplomatic as they collected my brother's shoes and helmet from the shoulder. I looked into the ambulance and saw a big blonde girl crying on a stretcher, asking for a phone. I handed her mine and crawled back out.

My parents looked young under the flashing police lights. They were dressed just like the Polaroids on Dad's desk. One was a closeup of my mom's face the moment he asked her to marry him on top of Mount Audubon. Her cheeks were sunburned. Blonde hair blowing across a relieved smile, squinting in the sun. The second picture was taken with a tripod. My parents held each other against the high Rocky Mountain winds, and the piece of paper in my dad's hands was blown against itself, folded like a letter. My mom told me that piece of paper was a photo of me. I was three years old in the photo, with two pigtails fastened with fluffy white scrunchies. *Masha, 1993.* My dad proposed to her with a triangle-cut diamond and a child who could be flown out from Nizhny Novgorod at a week's notice. My mom had her tubes tied at 28 after a traumatic late-stage DNC. She never regretted her abortion until they adopted my brother.

Every Christmas, my parents received a blue envelope stamped POCHTA ROSSII. Inside was a postcard and printed photos of all their adoptable children. One of them was Mark, a 6 year old with doe eyes and a buck toothed smile.

"He's adorable," my mom cooed. "And we can fix those teeth."

After the second time my brother locked me in the trunk, my parents started sending me to a therapist, a spindly crone who pulled her feet up on her chair with her knees up to her chin. She'd draw her legs up like that, peering at me from over her clipboard, holding it like a shield. She reminded me of a spider. She began and ended the sessions with a reminder to never say any of this to any adult from school. Her eyes flew open when I told her that my mom thinks my brother is the demonic reincarnation of her aborted baby. She scribbled on her pad in a frenzy and chewed through her pen and I was never taken to see her again.

The blonde girl had gotten blood all over my phone. I wondered if any of it was my brother's. I wondered if my brother and I were blood related. Littermates. Was Mark born with his compulsions? Or was it the dental anesthesia that did him in? Hours of gas pumped into his 7 year old brain, just to close the gap between his teeth. The tiny pink chasm that he'd show off whenever he drank out of a straw.

I wiped the blood off onto my shirt and joined my parents.

Swimming Lessons in a Dead Nepenthe

Smooth channels between painted bricks connect the wall where I rest my feet. They never turn the lights off in here.

Yesterday they took me out of solitary to meditate with a woman from Iowa who was trying to tell me I can Transcend my way out of here. I'm supposed to trust her. After all, she Transcended her way out of Iowa.

I watch my bent knees and feet planted on the wall and flip the prison in my mind. The wall is a floor now. I'm walking to the sink. I'm in my white kitchen. I'm pouring a drink.

Ashes. Ammonia. Blue Monday. Black January. The spies in the cement between your bathroom tiles love this time of year. Lock, caulk, and barrel. They place bets on your head, betting against the chance the impulse will die in your bed. They go all in on your death drive, the drive to change your state of matter; slit your wrists, cut your hair, dissolve yourself into a sludge for someone else to scrape off the bathtub after you're gone. They watch you with mildew eyes, their shekels sweating in their pockets as they bet on the evergreen hunger implied on boxes of commissary hair dye:

Autumn Flame, Burnt Umber, Cardamom Rye

I knew a guy who prefers blondes. They're the first thing he thinks of when he skydives. He's shacking up with the only barmaid in his Alaskan town because he hasn't read *The Castle*.

He'll jump out of a plane and fuck a bottle blonde but turn his nose up at a machine-rolled cigarette.

There are books in here that were blotted with K2 and LSD, pages ripped out to roll up and smoke. Fiercely guarded in the library, appropriately hidden among the fantasy novels and self-help.

My great-grandfather said it took a month for loose skin to start appearing around the Gulag. It hung down their thighs like dresses, keeping them modest. That's how you could tell who used to be rich on the outside. Fate is always finding ways to preserve their dignity. A velvet carpet unrolled down to the Fourth Circle of Hell. All the way to Plutus' boot clamping down on the final edge, the part that curls up a bit, never laying flat.

Dolores O'Riordan went swimming with her friends and never made it out of the water— a great way to die, we agreed. That was how I remembered it. That's how they harvest Cranberries.

New Englanders in rubber waders flood the bog and skim the red berries that float to the top. There's something joyfully pagan about that method of harvest. But the truth is, Dolores died in her hotel room in London. She drank too much and drowned in the bath. Everything comes down to the vessel, everything comes down to volume.

The song I hear through the walls sounds better the further they turn the dial. Right, right, right— there.

The broken speaker sounds right once a day when Hank Williams comes on the radio after dinner. Life in mono. Mono, *mono*, monkey business. When the woman from Iowa started on the Enlightened Ape business I started to picture her as a chimpanzee. Her elongated philtrum began to expand, her hairline dropped lower, her skin thickened, her eyes darkened, her voice grew shrill and inhuman. I began to feel a profound sense of nausea.

Hiram Williams and Robert Matthew Van Winkle, Hank and Vanilla: same spoon, different soup. Southern boys with rap sheets and head injuries. I wish I could fall asleep for 20 years.

In med school my mom dissected a thin female cadaver who erupted barely digested packet ramen noodles under her scalpel. A Japanese surprise, a Pearl Harbor of the mind. I could picture it perfectly. I never touched the stuff before I came here.

I steady ice on my tongue until it's the same temperature as my mouth, skin, cheeks, blood, spit. It tastes like the sensory deprivation tank in Portland.

Can the pressure in my stomach ever be as strong as the Mariana Trench?
    Subaquatic. Millions of tons of salt, water, acid, currents.
    What happens when you throw a knife across the Atlantic?
    Does it boomerang and land in a pile of sludge between New York and New Jersey?

And what did Jim Sullivan know about a UFO?

I could be 16 the way they sucked down my ID with the smallest bit of adrenaline. Looking me up and down. I could always tell they were the slightest bit eager to see something fake.

Bamboo groves grow like gentle Asian strokes but their papery leaves will slice you up if you're running fast enough. Their red calligraphy mocks my skin like an impulsive tattoo. A poor translation in a strip mall. The cuts took weeks to heal.

Applying makeup breaks down to the concepts of shadow, light, contrast, and concealment.

If the red and blue are flashing LED, and the white is still and opaque, you didn't run fast enough.

If you turn and see the highway moving without you, you may have lost the race.

If you call someone you hate for a favor, they might be so surprised they can't say no.

Every night the tiles in this tiny room are backlit by lamps fit for an Olympic pool and did you know sleeping in the true dark prevents insulin resistance? This is more *White Nights* and *Notes from the Underground*

than *Notes from the House of the Dead.*
You wouldn't let me cross the lake although I'm a good swimmer. Besides I've tried to die three times but the current was never quite taken with me. I've always felt Pan watching me with his thick thighs flattened on a chair his gold chain swinging like a big cloying Calder mobile taunting

grab it

l'enfant

The angels catch you early if they feel there's hope. They put their angel fingers on the cheeks of the man who catches you and gives you that look. They twist his neck towards you, and his eyes say, *put it back. Go home.*

I'd never been arrested before
   I run I float I swim I look the part I look 14 15 16 17 18 19

Catch is good, catch is crab nets and buttered lobster and acrobat twins in perfect rhythm. *Caught* is learning how to swim among the other fish with hooks in their lips and numbers on their sleeves and *caught* is taking

swimming lessons in a dead nepenthe, in the gunmetal prison toilet hitched to the wall, shaped like the silver spoon I've been trying to pass, shaped like a dead poison pitcher plant that's lost its rank in the jungle. A cold Duchamp turned right side up to keep me company. A Rubbermaid of Jungle Juice, a trough of holy water, a deer-sized freezer, a refrigerator full of dead kids in Novgorod, Florida, or Kyrgyzstan, and

when they baptized my ex sister in law her christening gown went clear and showed everyone the goblin tattooed on her chest and

my cat will eat whatever you give him as long as it's outdoors.

Catch a Fade

I COULD TELL he'd been to the barber earlier that day— the cheap place by his apartment. I could tell by the way the Dominicans gerrymandered his Caucasian hairline, shaving his widow's peak clean off. The edge of his Pushkin-length beard was shaved seamlessly into his sideburns, a perfect curve, as if done with a compass. He looked like a Syrian cab driver in the dark. It made me laugh so hard I tripped while he was dragging me outside of the Polish embassy. My arm disappeared in his grip, wide palms and the long, calloused fingers of a painter.

I laugh when I'm nervous, I can't help it.

I could only *partially* blame the Dominicans.

I counted six black SUVs parked around Observatory Circle, all filled with Balkans who wouldn't do a thing if they saw him put his hands on me.

He took my chin in his hand and reached to rub my lipstick off with his sleeve.

"Stop. It'll look messy."

"Can't get any worse."

"I need to get back to work."

"Get back to work," he repeated. Now it was *his* idea.

Russians are close talkers, but Germans like to get even closer. I backed into the buffet table and my palm fell into a platter of hors d'oeuvres— meat wrapped in meat, the tray superfluously decorated with fresh greens. The film professor didn't notice. He kept talking Haneke as I emptied a fistful of bacon into a napkin and dropped it in the trash.

I caught my reflection in a samovar and wondered if he was right about the lipstick.

Jersey Devil's Breath

Every winter, the Jersey Shore freezes into an old car in the driveway, tarped and bricked until May. Spiders start to crawl indoors for warmth, skittering across your ceiling, getting a lay of the place. Everyone walks into my pharmacy looking like a neglected baseboard, dry flaky skin and pilled acrylic sweaters. Their noisy coats, complete with velcro patches full of lint and ski passes from 2013, start to crowd my plexiglass cell. I pass the time by trawling for girls with a flush in their cheeks, a slapped-around vulnerability, like that girl in V/H/S. Kate Lyn Sheil face. Girls who look like they've been treading water.

Once in a while, the fog clears up and the sun casts relentless daylight that none of these women are ready for. They've been losing their Vitamin D indoors in their layers, beanies hiding their oily roots. Rubbed raw by the dry air, they look like they've been crying. It keeps them busy.

They're exhausted from days of writing Herzen novels on the backs of their eyelids— *Who is to Blame?* Ophelias floating on their backs, reaching for driftwood and lilypads and messages in bottles. Decision fatigue. Hypnosis. A row of women in latex caps waiting for a whistle. But even if something was able to pierce their catatonia they wouldn't admit it. They're comfortable as koi; their mouths open and undiscerning, swallowing all the different ways their fate can be repackaged, renovated, and resuscitated: astrology, tarot, true crime, SSRIs, benzodiazepines, amphetamines, contraceptives…

Some of the women that come into the pharmacy have that wrapped-in-paper look. Fresh from bad news at the doctor, or worse: just given a clean bill of health. I picture them in scant paper gowns shivering under fluorescent lights. I can hear them shifting on a strip of taut paper, how it rips and creases. They crinkle like deli Reubens while they lament fatigue, weight gain, mood swings, cramps, thinning hair, thinning eyebrows, brittle nails, and sensitivity to cold. They're given a vague diagnosis, if any. Usually one of the three horsemen of estrogen dominance: endometriosis, Hashimoto's, or PCOS. These low-iron ShopRite Botticellis leave the doctor's office with the only solution given to women like them: birth control. The doctor wouldn't dare tell them to lose weight, go for a walk, quit the $8 Barefoot chardonnay, no —

Better to sterilize them with synthetic estrogen that raises tissue copper levels, and depletes their zinc and B12. Better to poison them with heavy metals that make them even more paranoid, isolated, and driven to self soothe with drugs and carbs and buying shit off Etsy. Back in the '70s, they'd be stamped a *histapenic schizophrenic* and shipped off to McLean. But now, they hide their dry skin and weight gain under black cotton and foldover waistbands while they vent on the internet where they talk each other into applying for medical cards.

I want to catch one of these women in the early stages of her metamorphosis. I'm fly fishing for the last girl in Tom's River who hasn't become a stoner shut-in and gained the agoraphobia 80, but my waders are starting to chafe. I want to look over and see my wife in the passenger seat, seatbelt dividing her breasts, tiny blue veins waiting for me, watching me run in to buy her folic acid. I can find the prenatal vitamins with my eyes closed. I'm back in moments, but she already misses me and keeps her fingertips on the back of my neck until we pull into the driveway.

The dating apps are too eager, too constructed. They're for men who don't know where to look:

/r/astrology	*/r/MorbidReality*
/r/autoimmune	*/r/offmychest*
/r/BPD	*/r/PMDD*
/r/CPTSD	*/r/relationships*
/r/EDrecovery	*/r/selfharm*
/r/endo	*/r/stopdrinking*
/r/fibromyalgia	*/r/trees*
/r/Jung	*/r/truecrime*

/r/LetsNotMeet   */r/tumblr*
/r/loseit   */r/vegan*
/r/meditation

Sometimes I even scroll the r4r's until I can't take it. Every post is a skunky, desperate flicker of butane. Every local r4r is a landfill of abandoned accounts (because anyone sane uses a throwaway they've forgotten the password to by morning). Just sleep it off, people. The few women who post there are stray dogs, rifling through bins for something bone-shaped. They're field hockey women, charging in wet mouth guards that make their philtrums jut out like apes. Safety pins line the bottoms of their kilts.

I've learned plenty from whale watching at the pharmacy; I get to know a woman's full name, age, address, and what drugs she's on. But it turns my stomach. I miss fixing laptops in the Rutgers library. Girls would give me their whole computer for three days, treats on my snout. I started buying these cute animal-shaped rubber flash drives that they sold by the register in the student union Starbucks.

A duck for Yasmin, the blonde girl with thick Dutch lips and legs.
   A cow for Vidhi, the Indian pre-med with silky hair down to her hips.
   A fox for Marion, the tattooed French girl addicted to video games.

I wonder how campus looks this year. Back then, it was full of girls with long hair parted to the side, big sweaters and low heeled boots that went up their thighs like stockings. I miss the view from my office, the river of girls, blissfully ignorant of their active cases of ringworm or Crohns or psychosis.

*

My boss, Pat, thought changing our name from *Route 9 Pharmacy* to *Garden State Apothecary* would cut down on the recent break-ins.

"*Apothecary* makes it sound like we don't keep anything harder than Valerian."
   Apothecary makes it sound like we carry kratom and rose quartz dildos, but nobody consulted me.

The name change has been Y2K for our biggest demographic: the seniors of Leisure Village, wheeled in by their caretakers that only come in three types; underachiever alt girls with thigh tattoos, middle aged Nigerians, or one of their angry, impatient, and exhausted adult children. They relax when they hear me, good old Tom, explain *yes, this is the same pharmacy you've been coming to for the past decade, Ethel.* Being right downstream of seniors ensures we get the most gorgeous cornucopia of drugs: ambien, scopolamine, and every painkiller in every form: liquid, patches, and pills.

The foster mom of five comes in with a kid too old to be sleeping in a stroller. His legs hang over the side. There's an orange Jergens stain on her sweatshirt collar year round. I fill three bottles of Risperidone and try to forget she exists.

I swear menopause is just another form of demonic possession.

The young women who come in tremble like deer as they tell me their name and birth date. I like to say their addresses a little *too* loudly so I can watch them check over their shoulders in a panic. They get flustered and fumble with their tote bags when it's time to pay. Women under 40 don't carry wallets anymore. Some girls turn so I can't see into their purses, while others set their makeup, hair ties, tampons, notebooks, rolling papers, and receipts onto my counter while searching for their debit cards. *Perverts.* When girls are lowering their voices to tell me their government names, I wonder if they'll think of me later while they're mixing my Xanax with vodka. I give them my canned warnings about drug interactions and try not to stare at the bottle openers on their key rings while they stand there and nod and lie. They lie like I didn't see them stealing Revlon before they got in line. So I savor the timid way they look at me when they come to pick up their antifungals, their antibiotics, their antipsychotics; the way their chins tuck away and their eyes dart under my shark belly because they know I know *everything* about them.

Today a girl's backpack swung into the sunglass rack as she cut in front of the line. No one bothered to correct her. None of the queued up seniors and diabetics and opiate addicts even noticed. They're so lethargic you could sew six of them into one of those gigantic denim couches that rot in American basements. She rushed up to me with her deep voice and dark bloodshot eyes, dark haired, nervous, and pale as an ash. Chapped lips and last night's makeup.

Laura Meade
10/4/1991
Seroquel
Norethindrone
Flagyl
Clonazepam

In places too far north for grapes to grow, Finns and Vikings fermented yeast and honey into a scratchy sweet liqueur that kept them drunk through the winter. Mead loosened the hand that wrote Beowulf. Aristotle's, too.

I stared at her tongue while she fidgeted and struggled to pronounce her prescriptions. It's not white. Maybe the fungus is on her feet. Or maybe the Flagyl is for those ruddy cheeks hiding under dark side bangs. She wears too much black for her complexion. Ripped tights under shorts and someone else's baggy sweatshirt. The little glimpses of her legs were bright pink from the cold.

"Can you say that one more time?"

She turned and sized up the people waiting behind her. She leaned over the counter and repeated herself, giving me a smell of her cinnamon gum and musky perfume. I wanted to see what was in that backpack, but her cards were ready in her coat pocket.

"Do you have any questions for the pharmacist?"
  "Can I have my ID back?"

I love how girls always say *can* you, like they know I could just keep it. I do sometimes, if they don't ask. They're so grateful when they come in the next day, glowing with relief and thanking me for finding their ID and saving them a trip to the DMV. I pulled the card from under my keyboard and handed it to her, letting her tug it a little. She looked much younger than her age; heart shaped face, tight jawline, the kind of girl who gets carded everywhere. Maybe she was a little hungover and needed it to go find the hair of some dog. She shoved the paper prescription bags inside her coat and stomped out of the pharmacy, never giving me a glimpse into that backpack.

Laura's phone number and address, warm from the printer, rode shotgun on my way home. The address led to an office park with the names of four Jews and an Armenian printed on a large glass sign. I sat in my car wondering if she was being sneaky or just spaced out when she put her doctor's address as her own.

Plan B came to me halfway through my shift at work the next day. I called House of Paint from the parking lot and put a pair of navy blue coveralls on hold. I wanted to ask 'Betty' if they named their store after the wiggers who wrote *Jump Around* but she hung up.

The canvas coveralls hung over my headboard, making my room smell like a camping chair. I wonder what Laura looks like in a sleeping bag. A simple search of her name revealed a disappointingly sterile online presence. Blurry concert footage, sunsets, other people's pets.

I charged one of my burner phones and drafted her a text:

> A Sears Home Warranty technician will arrive tomorrow, 10/17/2015, 7:00-9:00 AM for scheduled maintenance. Please reply to this message with a photo of your washing machine's model number located inside of the door.

iPhone users never change their exif settings. All I needed was a photo.

She responded quickly, with two pictures. A blur and a redo. And now I know she lives in a vinyl sided split-level in Brick Township with overgrown sweetgrass in the front yard.

My roommates were in the kitchen mixing drinks and using every inch of counter space. Ryan, Paul, and Mikey are in a 90s cover band called *Shiver Phoenix (RIP)*. They sound like shit and come home from shows with $40 in a mason jar and girls who tag along like rain soaking the hems of their baggy jeans. I don't know how Ryan came to own this house, or keep it. Rent's cheap.

Ryan was leaning against the kitchen counter shirtless in unbuttoned jeans and one red sock. He never wears anything under his jeans and I can see a fleur-de-lis of golden pubes underneath his thumb ring. His hooded eyes make him look permanently stoned and secretive, and once in a while a girl will tell him he looks *exactly* like David Gilmour. Sure, he's got Gilmour's eyes and hair, but he also has those *jowls* everyone from central Jersey seems to have. They hide under his sandy beard, but I see them.

One of the girls they tracked into the house tonight is a loud Filipina in a Monmouth hoodie. She keeps crossing and uncrossing her muddy sneakers on the arm of the couch. She's yelling at her drunk friends as they struggle with the sliding door and slam their palms on the glass, the same way seniors bang on my pharmacy window at 6:57 AM.

I need to get my leftovers from the fridge but Paul's leaning against it. He was pulling out all the stops for a mixed girl in volleyball shorts, feeding her strips of bread dipped in ShopRite chipotle olive oil and telling her he infused it himself. There's an orange stain on his poncho and I can see her staring at it, covering her mouth while chewing, waiting for him to stop talking. She was a whole head taller than him. Ryan calls him Paul Simon when he isn't around. They call me Tom Jones to my face.

My crystal glass was in the sink and full of dried red crust— someone had used it to drink V8. Both ice trays were empty. I grabbed my bottle of gin out of the freezer and wrapped a rubber band an inch below the glass neck. *Snap.* That's my limit. I have to wake up early and pretend to do manual labor tomorrow.

*

I waited in my car until 7:15 AM. She'd never believe I'm a Sears guy if I came on time. Laura picked up on the third call.

"Basement's unlocked out back," she mumbled and hung up.

I put on my cap and a 3M mask and walked around the side of the house, hoping there were no men around. I dreamed this was some kind of sorority of knocked-out women. I imagined every soft surface in the house draped with pale legs and long hair, silent as kelp. At high and low tide, the women stir to take their seafoam green Clonazepams and go back to sleep.

I took a moment to sit on one of the patio chairs near the basement door before going inside. When I stood up, the frayed rattan caught on my sleeve, leaving white paint flecks on my new coveralls. I hate the mid-Atlantic attachment to wicker. There is no justification for dowdy, withering, impractical outdoor furniture. Don't they know they're being sold a byproduct? Giant piles of rattan ballast, discarded from cargo ships, would lay around ports until a shrewd Bostonian turned it into furniture and carriages. A real life Rumplestiltskin. I set a timer on my watch.

The washing machine was surrounded by a moat of black jersey and neon lace. Everything was black except the underwear. Everything was cotton except the underwear. Dumb little Laura. I checked the pockets of her hoodies and jackets and shoved a few receipts into my coveralls. A pale green thong fit right in my chest pocket, but I took it back out, knowing whatever I'd take, I'd never get to see against her skin, cutting into her hips, pulled to the side. The floor above my head started to creak. An electric kettle clodded back onto its stand and the fridge squealed open and shut. Heavy steps started to come down the staircase. Bare feet, dolphin shorts, David Blaine t-shirt, and finally her face came into view.

I swear I saw her face painted on a lacquer box when I was a child. Symmetrical strokes of black, white, and pink that stared back at me in the window of an antique store.

"Are you done?"

Her voice was even huskier than yesterday. She seemed like one of those people who needed to be archaeologically excavated from bed.

"Just finishing up in the basement. I'll check your kitchen appliances next."

"If I need to pay for something, email it to my uncle Roger."

"Today's service is a complimentary routine maintenance as part of your Sears…"

She went back upstairs.

I did some Wim-Hof crouched in the moat of panties and leggings and band shirts and dug my fingernails into my palm one by one. *Cars, phone, computer.*

She was sitting cross legged at a formica card table that wobbled when I came into the kitchen.

"I'll be done in 10. Does this house have radiators, central heating, or compressed air?"

"Central, I think." She rubbed her eyes and looked at her fingertips. The corners of her eyes were full of black goo. *You really never wash your face, do you?* "There are vents in the floors."

"Mind if I take a look? We're having a cold snap next week."

She shrugged and took a loud sip of coffee. The bag of grounds was open on the counter, fallen on its side and making a mess.

"I'm going to have to check the bedrooms. Is anyone else home?"

"Just me."

I turned away so she wouldn't see the relief in my eyes. The Jeep and Impala winked at me from the driveway. We're old friends now. They're in on it. They're hiding magnetic GPS trackers in their wheel wells. I'm guessing either car could be hers, but I know she prefers the Jeep. Women love SUVs, Hummers, Jeeps, and Ford F-150s that they can't park. Cars they can barely get in and out of. A few months ago, a bobbed woman in big sunglasses and a Chevy Tahoe rear ended me in the Wawa parking lot. When it comes to jackets and cars, all women are crossdressers.

The first bedroom was covered in folded men's clothes, camping equipment, and cardboard boxes. The second was an office. The third was Laura's, reeking of her perfume and that synthetic vernix that covers everything you take home from the mall. Her carpeted room had one window and a pepto-bismol colored bathroom. Her laptop was open on the floor. I locked myself into the bathroom with it. I heard her pacing through the kitchen and didn't risk taking time to look behind her bathroom mirror. I had a good idea what was in there.

I came home to the satisfaction of seeing Ryan's cheek rub against the dirty arm of the couch. He was half asleep watching TLC with an ashtray on his chest.

"What's with the Dickies?"
  "They're comfortable."
  "You look like a plumber. You get fired from the pharmacy, Jonesy?"
  "Hey, have you ever been to this bar in Asbury Park? It sounds familiar." I showed him one of Laura's receipts.
  "It's one of the only good spots around here. We play there sometimes. I send you Facebook invites and you never come." He contorted his face into a little pout.
  "I'll come to the next one."
  "Doubt it. Why are you asking me about receipts?"

Ryan's laptop was permanently plugged in and open. Its broken fan fills the kitchen with white noise and heat. The only time it's ever closed is when someone's insomniatic one night stand patters into the kitchen and slams it shut. I pulled up his Facebook and invited Laura to SPRIP's next show. He'd invited 382 people. A drop of Meade in the bucket.

Laura was having a bad time at the concert. She had the shoulders of a girl just trying to stay out of the way. Not in line, not in the crowd, not at the bar. A t-shirt looped through the strap of her backpack and a beer in her hand. Her hair was washed and brushed but she kept twirling her ends until they looked stringy. I hate live music. I hate hearing people sing; it makes me feel embarrassed for them. I can't see the t-shirt under her arm. If she bought an SPRIP shirt I'll strangle her with it. Our basement is full of boxes of them. When girls lose their tops doing whatever they all do down there, Ryan throws them one and they act so grateful. They walk around in nothing but those big shirts like a Cult of the Gildan Dawn.

I couldn't think of anything to say to her so I thought of how to get some leverage. I went behind the merch table and asked her if she'd paid for the shirt. I repeated myself, louder, but she kept twirling her hair and looking at the light fixtures.

I followed her to the bar. She recrossed her legs and angled them away from me. Ryan clapped a hand on my back and I adored him for a moment.

"You made it!" He wrapped his arm around me and introduced himself to Laura. "Are you coming to the firepit after this?"

There were only five chairs around the fire. A tiny olive-skinned girl was sitting on Laura's lap and showing off a necklace she bought at Red Rocks, a sliver of pinecone encased in resin. Laura and Jenna rattled off festivals they've been in that ecstatic way girls talk to other drunk girls they've just met. I got up to get her a coat.

I sprayed cologne around the collar of my shearling jacket, wishing I'd listened to the gypsy girl at the Macy's perfume counter. She had me pegged as part Armenian almost immediately. She threw darts of what sounded like Russian and Farsi at me and cooed when I shook my head, *just English*. She pulled out perfumes in black bottles that promised tobacco and leather and cardamom, with words like *guilty* and *wanted* printed in gold. I didn't know how to tell Layla I didn't want to smell like an Arab and asked her what American girls buy for their boyfriends. She rolled her eyes. "There's always Armani and Polo."

"I noticed you were shivering." I put the jacket around Laura's shoulders and asked her if she wanted another beer.
   "Bring *me* another," Jenna interrupted.

"Trade School Tom! What happened to the Dickies? Did you guys see that the other day? This man came home donning some Dickies, you *had* to see it." Ryan nuzzled his beard into my neck as I stared into the refrigerator. "Nice find, by the way."
   "You should go for the tan one, with the pinecone around her neck. She's cute."
   "We'll leave it up to the girls, huh?" He clapped me on the back on his way out. I thought about the safe in my room, and what I could put into his White Claw. No benzos, he's worked up a tolerance. Maybe

something sitcom and crass, like a laxative.

I've never looked into Ryan. It's just that he looks like a guy who might have a pierced cock that he's proud of, and I don't want to stumble upon that. I've intercepted check-thin envelopes from a woman with the same last name. A Merchantville address. I've thought to look her up but then I think of all the jowls and the impulse evaporates quickly.

Through the window I could see a different girl wearing my shearling jacket. I was sobering up and starting to lose my nerve. I imagined the sound of Laura moaning under Ryan muffled through six inches of plaster, mere feet from my head. I couldn't change the tape. The idea of them fucking rattled in my head like keys trapped in a dryer.

My safe is hidden behind strategically chopped and glued Franzen and Patterson hardcovers from the thrift store. I keep my burner phones and menagerie of flash drives in there, as well as amphetamines, opiates, benzodiazepines, abortion pills, beta blockers, and edibles. Everything I could steal from the pharmacy before Pat got too keen to our 'break-ins'. I wonder if he suspects me. Even so, a man like Pat? Any minor social friction floods his engine. He'd rather deal with insurance for months than cops for hours.

The girl wearing my jacket made a fuss when I asked for it back. When she took her phone out of my pocket, a folded sheet of printer paper slid out with it. Laura saw me snatch it from her.

"What was that?" She squinted her eyes and swayed in front of me. She smelled like vanilla and woodsmoke and her house. I loved knowing what her house smells like.

"Work stuff. Private."
   "Tom's a fed!" Jenna yelled.
   "Tom's a pharmacist," Ryan corrected her. "And he takes privacy very seriously. Hungry hungry HIPAA."

Laura wandered into my next door neighbor's yard, into Gabe's forgotten pile of lawn flamingos. She pierced the ground with each of their spokes, setting them upright in a ring. She threw her jacket off inside the circle and laid down, putting chapstick on in wider and wider concentric circles, down to her chin. She looked drunk enough to piss herself.

"Do you have a lighter?" she mumbled, before pulling a yellow Bic out of her coat and thanking herself. She put the business end of her cigarette in her mouth and struggled with the flint with that little black thumbnail bitten down to the quick. I helped her up. Her palms were so soft it was almost disgusting.

We watched my backyard from Gabe's. The fire was dying down and Jenna was ringing a bell she'd found in the kitchen. She was sitting in Ryan's lap, her long black hair fanned out over his bare chest.

"I can feel my nose getting numb."
   "If it was numb, you wouldn't feel it."
   "Can you drive me home?"

"End of the month. Cops are out."

She ripped one of the flamingos out of the soft ground and walked back to the firepit.

"Tom hates cops."
   "Tom hates everything." Ryan intercepted the flamingo before Laura could feed it to the fire.

The girl who was wearing my jacket walked up to me and touched my chin. "You look like this guy I saw on TV."
   "An actor?"
   "No, a guy on Forensic Files. He killed a girl's whole family, even her dog, and stuffed their bodies in a hollow tree. He held her captive in his house full of leaves, just bags of leaves all over the floors and stacked up the walls. He was *obsessed* with leaves."

I started to feel a little paranoid. *House of Leaves* was one of the thrift store books I butchered to create the panel in front of my safe.

"He *begged* the cops not to cut the tree down. That's how much he loved nature."

"You do kinda look like Matthew Hoffman." Laura smirked.
"Now *you're* in on this?"

I hoped Laura was drunk enough for that to sound playful. Women can't drive or figure out their taxes, but have an encyclopedic knowledge of serial killers. I looked the guy up on my phone. Ohio physiognomy. Receding hairline. I went inside for a hat.

The girls followed me inside like ducks. Ryan herded them downstairs to play cards. He renovated the basement last summer in anticipation of needing a place to bring girls when the firepit gets too cold. He even hung fairy lights and one of those hippie harem tapestries from Amazon. I've seen girls get so drunk down here it makes me wonder if they know they're in a gingerbread house for groupies and not their dorm rooms. I can't stand to be down here for too long.

The next morning I went back downstairs before anyone else woke up. I stared at the two of them intertwined on the big denim couch near the dryer and thought of the first time I'd seen her: the sound of the sunglass rack and her hoarse voice. Hungover sweat tickled my ribs and my Ativan hadn't kicked in yet. He didn't even *try* last night. All it took was being the last two people awake in the basement. I waited for her white Jeep to disappear from our driveway before venturing out of my room again. Ryan had just woken up and was half naked in the kitchen.

"Were you crying earlier, Jonesy?"
  "No."
  "Porn?"
  "Yeah."
  "I swear to god I heard you crying but Mikey said you were probably just watching something."
  I ignored him and took out the eggs, butter, and hot sauce.
  "You know you can always come talk to me. My door is always open."

His door *is* always open.
  It leaks smells and sounds and glimpses of his hairy legs and surfer's ass as he slips into one of two pairs of low rise jeans that smell like Guantanamo Bay. Sometimes as I'm walking to the bathroom at night, I see Ryan with an unfamiliar girl curled up on his chest while they

watch one of three shows on his laptop: Walking Dead, Entourage, or The Wire. He always waves at me as I pass and the girl flinches to cover herself and I look down at the ex-white carpet under my feet and I'm too nervous to pee once I get to the bathroom.

"You don't think I slept with her, do you?"

I thought about my safe.

"Bro code, Jones. We just cuddled."

I believed him. If he scored he would have dangled that shit in my face.

*

The only thing Laura has in common with my roommates is that they never have anywhere to be. She started coming over a few times a week to smoke their weed and raid our fridge and go to thrift stores and fill our house with vintage ashtrays and framed paintings of forest animals and other junk. They've bought pillows and easy chairs and beanbags that could barely fit in her Jeep. They make bonfires every night. They've burned every stick in every yard down our block. She dug through everyone's trash and burned every cardboard box, every receipt, every scrap of paper she could find. She says that's what her family used to do. Ryan told me she comes from Polish stock. Camdenites. Trash burners.

I came home from work to Laura sitting cross legged on the living room carpet, crying. Ryan and Mikey were sprawled out on the beanbags, doing their best to appear concerned.

"For weeks I've had this bad feeling, like I'm being followed. And then I found this."

On the coffee table, next to the new ashtray, was one of the GPS tags.

"Back in July, she was driving with her brother when he lost control of the car and slammed into a church. He lost consciousness, and she ran into the basement to get help. She borrowed a car from someone in that NA meeting and ended up denting it in the hospital parking lot. Now that junkie's trying to sue her, months later, out of nowhere." Ryan told me the whole story without even craning his neck. Sounds like he'd heard her blubber out this story a couple times this afternoon and was trying to cut to the chase.

I crouched next to her like a camp counselor. "This could have been planted by a PI, insurance claims investigator, or a lawyer looking for evidence." I picked up the tag and dropped it back on the table like a coin. "This is a desperate move. An intimidation tactic, even. You should just throw it into the Atlantic."

She put the tag back into her pocket. "Or burn it."

I was so relieved that I joined Laura on her nightly trespass for firewood. She unfolded our tarp a few doors down and covered it in sticks, pinecones, and fistfuls of leaves. At one house she waved to an old lady I'd never seen before, watching TV in her living room. Laura tried to start a sentence with me a few times, like a kid afraid of her parents. I wondered if I was supposed to offer to pull the tarp.

"So Ryan says you're a pharmacist?" Her voice tilted up. "What's that like, any fun?"

Any fun?

I wondered if she knew about me, how fun my job can be, how fun I make it. How I had too much fun when I was fixing laptops at Rutgers and got caught because Russians are the most paranoid fuckers on the planet. Polina Sherbakova stomped into the library five minutes before closing, looking for me. She stood there and hissed at me with that tongue, a carpet on the wall. I liked hearing my name from her mouth. *Tom Kasabian.* Her perfume smelled stronger than when she came to pick up her Dell a few hours before. She'd even put on higher heels before coming to confront me.

"I found some-sing on my hard drive."

"Our repairs come with a 30-day guarantee. If your device is still…"

"I know you fucked with my computer. And I don't trust you to remove it. You're going to buy me a new Macbook, or I'm calling the cops."

I had stayed up late the night before looking through her photos. I saw every way that she used her french tipped nails and bleached hair to tease me; hand bras and mermaid curtains. There were also family photos that showed me she had two brothers who were built like walk-in freezers so I gave her the money and quit.

Her flash drive is my favorite: the snow leopard.

"It's a job, I guess."

I went to the bathroom and looked up Laura's brother while the others built a fire. Squat rack videos and Kevlar-Oakley car selfies. Group photos with his cop dad and cop uncle.

Laura. The fucking infanta of a central Jersey cop dynasty. And I didn't even ask what the tracker was. The three of them saw me immediately identify it in the living room. *She could have been testing me.* Anyone in law enforcement can easily get Apple to tell them who bought it. I got it off eBay with an account tied to a burner email— but from my own IP address.

I drank a soapy Blue Moon and mentally inventoried my safe as I looked around the backyard. Mikey was asleep in his camp chair. Ryan was pissing malt liquor into the fire. Laura was breaking sticks on her knees. I could give them something that would make them all fall asleep and die peacefully in the cold. I could give them Ambien, car keys, and convince them to drive on the highway. I could gas them in the basement. Or I could fix some gin & tonics.

I went back inside and put Ryan's warm computer on my lap. I copied and pasted our address to the Filipina, Jenna, and a couple other women he's fucked. I couldn't think of a chaser and just closed the chats. I've seen him do more with less.

The girls didn't respond. After an hour I brought Mikey a blanket and Ryan a high dose of zinc. I told him it was ashwagandha. Once his guts were emptied out around the backyard, I suggested we go inside. I half-carried Ryan to his room and gave him what he hoped was Zofran.

"You're going to feel so much better, Ryan," Laura said over my shoulder, handing a glass of water down to our patient.

"She's right."

300mg of Demerol on an empty stomach will feel great for a few hours until he's knocked out for the night. Maybe longer. I tucked pillows under his arms and a towel under his neck so he couldn't roll over.

I went out back into a bamboo thicket on Gabe's property. I dug a hole one foot deep and buried my safe. I used my hands— I would not be seen with a shovel tonight. Gabe was watching TV. All our neighbors down this street are old and housebound. I wonder if they watch us.

I joined the others in the basement with a surprise and they eagerly swallowed the paper parachutes I'd prepared. Only Laura's had MDMA— Mikey and Paul would be passed out within the hour. I helped her up the stairs because the scopolamine patch I'd stuck on her back a few hours ago was starting to kick in.

Devil's Breath. Burundanga. Belladonna. An ancient, versatile cure for sufferers of motion sickness, seasickness, Parkinson's tremors, tight-lipped MK Ultra subjects, or postoperative nausea. It's popular among the hospice nurses at Leisure Village because it silences their patients' death rattles. Combined with morphine, scopolamine submerges a patient into twilight sleep; a state of no memory and no pain. Like two fat snakes twisting into one another, they produce an anesthetized, half-conscious, robotic state where a person can access their memories, but not their imagination. They can't go digging for a lie.

It was time for Laura's interview.

"Do you know who's been keeping an eye on you?"

"I *told* you guys. I got into an accident."

"You said you hit someone's car."

"I made a mistake. That's why I moved. My uncle has a house in Brick, he's never around. He's been taking cruises back to back since my aunt died. It might sound morbid, but that's what she told him to do with the life insurance."

"Sounds like a practical woman." I had forgotten the wicker furniture. "What did you do?"

"Sometimes my brother would let me drive the cop cars, unmarked Chargers. We love those cars, they remind us of the pitbull we grew up with. Muscly, low to the ground, keyed up. But I never really got used to that accelerator…"

She sat up and pulled my blanket around her. She had developed a relentless jaw tic from the MDMA that seemed to rock her whole body. I gave her a can of pink wine from the mini fridge I bought last week. I wasn't going to let her clam up.

"I love wine in a can." She flipped it open after a few tries.

I waited for her to take a few big sips. "Finish your story, Laura."

"One night, Greg and I were driving around Washington Township after a night out. We were doing a little drive-by. He wanted to check up on his ex. He just wanted to know which lights were on in her house, which cars were in her driveway, what was in her trash…"
     "And?"
     "Kitchen and bedroom, her Honda Fit, Michelob Ultra."
     "Was he angry?"
     "No, she was alone. It calmed him down a little. He let me drive home."
     "Did you get into an accident?"
     "I hit the accelerator too hard and crashed into a janitor who was leaving her shift at a church. The Charger was totaled so I took her keys out of her apron and drove Greg to the hospital in her van."
     "Were you injured?"
     "No. But Greg had a concussion."
     "Did they investigate the crash?"
She oozed down my bed like butter down toast, stopping at the crust. She looked up at me and pulled my hands over her face, down her neck. "Let's watch a movie."
     "Do you think anyone *else* is watching you?"
     "You're watching me right now," she whispered.
     "If you know, you need to tell me."
Her face contorted into a swollen grimace, like a soft fish ripped from 2,000 feet under the sea. She started to cry "*I can't go to prison,*" wailing over and over again. "Ever since I found that thing on my car, I've been afraid to be in my own house for too long. Afraid they're gonna arrest me. What if they've bugged Roger's house?"
     "We can check tomorrow. With or without you. I can pretend to be a Sears guy, in case someone is casing your house. They can't link us."
     "I think a fake Sears guy already came to my house a month ago. He

smelled good and he wasn't holding a clipboard."

"Did the nurses at the hospital see you that night?"

"We went to the hospital where my stepmom works. I called her on the way there."

The investigation was closed. The union gave Greg 24 hours to sober up before he got breathalyzed in the hospital. The Charger was compacted. The dented van was impounded, wiped down, and returned to the family. The Methodist church was ordered to cut down their hedges and construct a low cement wall around the parking lot. Greg's little sister was never with him that night.

"Do you have your Klonopin with you?"

"In my backpack. Want some?"

"Don't take it tonight. It doesn't mix." I took the wine out of her hand and gave her a carton of milk.

"How did you know I have Klonopin?" She poured the milk down her throat, getting it all over her face and chest. She handed me the empty carton and asked for more. I gave her water and hid her backpack under the bed. I held up a sweatshirt in one hand and a t-shirt in the other. She pointed to the sweatshirt and lifted her hands up obediently. Her arms, breasts, and ribs were covered in goosebumps.

"I want to take a shower." Her vowels could barely escape her clenched jaw.

"I know you're cold. Your body is just having a hard time calibrating. You can't take a shower yet, your body temperature will drop dangerously as soon as you get out."

"I'd rather die than go to prison."

I took her underneath my comforter and held her firmly as her body shook in my arms. I'd never comforted a woman before but I couldn't give her an Ativan on top of everything else. I gambled on the scopolamine, alcohol, and molly and hoped she'd remember the warmth of my chest and not what I was about to tell her: the truth.

I let her touch the canvas coveralls I'd hidden in a suitcase. Her face and shoulders melted once she realized no one had gotten wise to her DUI manslaughter. No one was coming to lock her up. She wasn't going to be the lone cop's daughter in Gloucester County Correctional. She curled into the fetal position and I could barely hear her last slurred whisper as she drifted into sleep:

"Tom, have you ever thought of becoming a cop?"

Skin in the Game

2044

ON MONDAY, Wednesday, and Thursday I sewed aprons, scrubs, and the gray uniforms that the COs wore. On Fridays I met with the psychiatrist who read my crimes back to me while I stayed mum. I'm told I was driving 130 mph on 95 and crashed into a bus full of Mormon missionaries with good attorneys. She told me Charlotte stayed back, waited for the cops, made sure to let them know her friend, who was driving, had run off, and probably needed medical attention.

I wasn't trying to give anyone a hard time. I really didn't remember that night. No hypnosis, meditation, or DBT could resurrect the memory of the joyride we took after the New Year's party. Hell of a way to start 2041. I only remember crawling out of the car through the left side window, running across the highway into a forest, breaking my nails on a brick retention wall, and scratching my legs on brambles and bamboo. The cops caught me in the parking lot of a furniture store, barefoot, covered in blood and a shredded cocktail dress.

The psych kept telling me how lucky I was to have a friend like Charlotte. So *involved* in my case, so hands on. So lucky to have a friend with a net worth rivaling the GDP of Belize. No one ever explained why I spent my first two years in Delaware when I crashed in Jersey and lived in New York. Hazel D. Plant Correctional was a blue and yellow facility built inside the clover of 95, encircled by the highway. The prison looked like it was born with its cord wrapped around its neck without anyone ever bothering to take it off. Nothing ever felt so bleak as being locked up in a prison painted like my high school in a state I wasn't sure anyone lived in. All I saw through the transport window was vinyl-sided factories and mowed medians. A white bus slowing at a bus stop without opening its door. No sidewalks, no churches. On the second Christmas inside I tried to kill myself with things I found in the janitor's closet but I snoozed through Chemistry so I just woke up with a sore esophagus and a new spot in Psych. They relocated me twice in Virginia until I ended up in her wilder little sister, in a facility by the Greenbrier River.

The psychiatrist followed me to Alderson and West Virginia was where she started on the hypnosis and transcendental meditation. I am easily hypnotized but cannot meditate to save my life. The psych says that disparity is common, that meditation is not as difficult for those who have trouble letting go as for those who have never held on in the first place. After 4 months I was told I'd made progress and after 6 I was told I'm getting out soon.

Charlotte scooped me out of jail in a white four-door pickup truck that smelled new. Her two kids were in the backseat, wearing similar hats knitted from different weights of yarn. Orange, white, purple, and turquoise stripes. All the scrap yarn I could find in the Fauquier County Corrections craft closet. The needles were made of a styrofoam that made a disgusting creak as they scraped together hats for Daisy, 12, and Bliss, 2. Acrylic, bamboo, aluminum, and steel needles were off limits. Ready made shivs. Less work than a toothbrush.

When we stopped at Walmart I saw the knitting needle situation wasn't so much better as a freedman. Embargos with Mexico over the Russian-Indian-Chinese-Brazilian-Mexican Alliance cut off American access to all the Susan Bates factories in Matamoros and Juarez.

"It's easy to babysit on the mountain. The house sits on a hill far above the treeline, nothing to block the view of the little runner. Keep Bliss in these crazy clothes, everything neon, and you can do it with one eye open halfway through the liquor cabinet."

I wonder if she forgot where the hats came from. She tried explaining that she and her husband were being tried for some minor white-collar crimes, frowned-upon reshuffling of funds. She used the word *scapegoat*. I couldn't quite understand what they'd done or if I could condemn it.

"Thanks for agreeing to watch the kids. Everything's fucked. My mom has to come back from Scotland, they won't let her teach this year. Accessory to my 'crimes'. Keith's waiting for me in New York, our trial starts Thursday. I don't want the kids living out of some hotel in the city. Too dangerous right now."

"I still don't get why Keith's parents can't take them."

"Molly's parenting philosophy is scheduling every single half hour of the day with a strictly enforced activity. She monitors bathroom breaks, meals, and playtime like the SS. No wonder Keith gained so much weight when he moved out. That's why he gambles, too. It's like a slingshot, the more you reign them in, the further they rebel."

"Kids rebel no matter how chill their parents were."

"You're a testament to that."

"Kids need structure."

"I won't send them to live with Molly." Charlotte checked that Daisy was far back in the cereal aisle and lowered her voice. "I'm afraid she'll give Daisy an eating disorder. She carefully measures out rice before she cooks it."

"That's how you cook rice, Char. You have to measure it to make sure the ratio of grains to water is correct."

"Really? I thought that was a calorie thing. I just pop Uncle Ben's into the microwave."

She piled boxes of minute rice, mac and cheese, and cake mix into her cart.

*

Charlotte's parents' mountain property was a stone house on six acres of land in Romney, West Virginia. Three of the seven bedrooms were used for storage. Clothes, cardboard, newspapers, magazines, holiday decorations, furniture, kitchen appliances that had never been unboxed. One of the bedrooms was refashioned into a walk-in closet, full of vintage dresses and fur coats preserved and climate-controlled at 49 degrees. The old house had no locks on the bedrooms. Half of the day was spent swatting Bliss away from those rooms where she loved to dig around for things to chew on and drop on her head. Daisy moved herself into the attic bedroom and hardly ever came out for air.

"You should go into town today. You're gonna go crazy with them after a few days. I need you to put on something bright and get *so* hungover that you don't even feel like going out for the next couple days. That's what I do."

I took her advice. I went to the clothes room and picked out a pair of white boots and a short Pucci dress. The polyester was coarse and thick; the zipper threatened to crack in my fingers.

Charlotte zipped me up and gave me the keys to her white pickup.

The first thing I did when I drove into town was put my finger on its pulse. Namely, eavesdrop on the old women at the deli counter.

"She's not a Gwyneth, she's a *Gwenette*."

"She humors me when I call her Gwyneth."

"I just call her Gwen."

"I'm worried about her, alone all these years. All she does is knit and smoke, knit and smoke. At night she goes on long walks with her dog."

"She's gonna get lost one of these days. Or hit by a car."

"Thank god she doesn't drive. She'd mow us all down."

"She's never driven a car. Her cowboy boots look like they've been hitched to a truck and dragged around since Neil Diamond had all his hair."

"Think he'll make it to 104?"

I left the diner and walked around the one-story town. The short brick buildings made me homesick; I get squirrely in places with height ordinances. I sat in front of the limestone bank, the biggest building I could find, before buying a movie ticket in the one-screen theater. The matinee was a film about a teenage guerrilla battalion in the mountains of Uruguay guarding the last dairy cow in South America. They shot it dead on the first night. I left the theater once they started skinning her.

It's good for a town to have one bar, takes out the guesswork. It's easier to meet people. I sat two seats down from an old man with long white hair and velcro sneakers. He turned to me and struck up a conversation.

"Skin— it's the new currency."

"That so?"

"People are selling cubes of skin to plastic surgeons. Funeral homes and the obese are making a killing. I was at my dermatologist the other day. He shares an office with a Dr. Jaw-lift Mengele. I opened up his binder, and it's just a catalog of skin, all colors. Like a paint guide at Home Depot."

"Did he catch you?"

"I wasn't snooping— he was selling me on it himself. Said I could look twenty years younger. I told him I was in prison twenty years ago and looked a lot worse than I do now."

"What's the skin for?"

"Skin grafts. Fake tits and phalloplasties. Neck lifts and face transplants. Height surgeries, too. They glue it on in strips. They shipped limestone from a quarry in Bedford, Indiana to build the Empire State Building. You get what I'm saying?"

"Sure."

He waved a hand in my face. Some kind of *youths of today* gesture. I turned to my left to see who else I could talk to. The bartender was staring at me from under her shiner, wiping someone's lipstick off a glass. I instinctively avoided her eye contact, dissecting her in my peripheral vision. She was tall and brunette, with a purple bruise covering the curve of her eye socket and cheekbone. She had tattoos peeking out of her long sleeves from every direction: on her wrists, neck, and collarbone.

"But it's more than skin deep," I heard the old man continue to the guy on his other side. "They're pushing the skin grafts on everyone, regardless of need. And to get a skin graft or transplant, you have to go through a nationally standardized protocol. Injections, pills, steroids, and immunosuppressives to prevent your body from rejecting the new skin as a foreign object. Toxic Shock Syndrome. Like when women keep their tampons in too long. Sometimes the skin just dies, it goes purple and green and starts to rot off the body. The pharmaceutical companies realized they could make a killing putting everyone on AIDS drugs by approving the off-label use. A cruel cycle. You ever wonder why the modern universal symbol for doctors is two SNAKES? Do you know anyone who did MAID? Assisted suicide? They're being kept alive for years. Their loved ones think they're dead, visiting fake gravesites all over the country. But they're really being held in facilities in Lynwood, Mableton, and New Rochelle, suburbs of LA, Atlanta, and NYC. Plastic surgery capitals of the US. They hold people in tanks that keep their skin moisturized and free of any diseases or blemishes."

"Wouldn't they get bedsores, laying around like that 24/7?"

"Are they conscious?" I asked, reentering the conversation.

"That's a question for Peter Singer."

"There's a prototype of the skin factories where the 'samples' are injected with scopolamine and Demerol and made to walk on treadmills for three hours a day. It improves the skin texture. That's how they made Madonna's third face transplant."

"I just listened to a podcast about skin grafts, Bill." The bartender interrupted. "It's dark, but juicy."

"Let's hear it, Melba."

"A woman was arrested in Virginia last week. Mitzy Katchman. She shared a duplex with a social worker named Pam Collins. Pam got fired from her job once they found out she'd been doing all of her house checks from her couch."

"Don't they all do that? She must have done something else. Like running up a big copay," Bill posited.

"*Bingo.* Pam sued, claiming they couldn't take away her health insurance, invoking some sort of Disability Act for her obesity. She won a hefty severance. Pam was doing okay, enjoying her free money and her busy social life, online, of course. Mitzy's half of the house was quiet. She lived alone with her preteen son, Rain, who stayed locked in his bedroom. One day when he was at school, she decided to snoop. She found stockings in his drawer and support groups in his open tabs. She started going on those same forums, pretending to be a trans teen herself. She started chatting with her son, bonding with him as 'Robin'. The further Rain transitioned, the more Mitzy's social life blossomed. Then came the two failed breast augmentations— necrosis, infection, total loss of skin. When she found out how much a skin transplant costs, she started to come up with a plan."

"Prostitution?"

"That wouldn't be in the papers." I interrupted. I wanted to hear where Melba's story was going.

"One day, Pam was smoking her bong on the back porch when Mitzy came out and asked her for a favor, some kind of help in the kitchen. It was the first sentence they'd exchanged in years. Mitzy had whittled away at one of the boards on her deck, working on it every day for weeks. She sanded and stripped one side, and flipped it over so that the top of it looked like the others. She guided Pam towards it, knowing she'd fall through the thin board and hurt herself. Pam managed to sprain both ankles. Mitzy helped Pam into her apartment, onto her couch, and announced that she was now her full time caretaker. Pam had just lost her job and her health insurance, and agreed to let Mitzy bandage her ankle instead of going to the hospital. She hid Pam's phone on top of her refrigerator and took the keys on her way out. Over the course of a month, she carved three-inch squares off her stomach, neck, and outer thighs, cauterizing the wounds with a clothes iron and freezing the swatches. They arrested her in the parking lot of the plastic surgery clinic."

A man in a NASCAR jacket appeared beside me, nodding to everyone at the bar.

"A pitcher for the corner booth?" Melba asked, scratching an inflamed tattoo on her chest. It looked fresh. I wondered if her tattoos protected her from skintheft. Maybe it made her more of a target. Maybe there were *collectors*, billionaires walking around in colorful human quilts.

"That thing on Melba's face isn't a shiner. It's a birthmark. It makes her look tougher than she is," NASCAR whispered to me as she filled a pitcher with her back to us. "For weeks I kept expecting it to heal. But she's never been in a fight."

She paused before handing the beer to NASCAR. She changed her mind, pulling it back, walking it to the booth herself. I turned to watch her bend over the table, arching her back in front of the group of bikers.

"She tried to be an actress but got laughed out of New York. Ran to West Virginia with her tail between her legs…"

Her stolen valor was starting to get under my skin. I bet her name isn't even Melba. Name changes have gotten really popular among the barista class. You can change your name and gender in ten minutes. The DMV website sends you a new birth certificate and you're off to begin your new life as Kish/Flax/Grae/Morrow. I met a woman named Tic in the deli this morning.

"Important beefs get figured out around the watering hole. Sometimes, even frozen beef gets thrown back into the microwave."
   "What?"

I gave NASCAR a quick once-over. He was oversharing, trying to lasso me into something. Maybe he was just forthcoming. He was attractive enough to just go up to women, maybe he never learned any better.

"Gox," he offered his hand.

I stopped myself from rolling my eyes but my tongue gave me away. "When'd you pick *Gox*?"

"My dad had these hiking boots that said Gox on them. I kind of liked how it sounds."

"You mean Geox?"

"Maybe, they were pretty old. Coulda been an *e* in there, rubbed off."

"What was your name before?"

"Do you want to join my table?"

I felt myself getting tight and reached into a basket of tots to soak up Melba's heavy pours. It was empty. Gox's friends all looked alike, pale skin and dark hair, tattoos, big fake leather racing jackets. His friend in the DuPont jacket leaned closer to me.

"Do you want me to order you some food?"

"Mozzarella sticks?"

When he got up I saw him limp a little, favoring his left leg. Another guy in a Busch jacket moved into his spot. Gox seemed aloof, or comfortable with how close his friends were getting to me. I couldn't comprehend their conversation. Something about cars, mileage, or real estate. DuPont came back with a basket of breaded mozzarella sticks.

"I'm Damon, by the way."

I winced at the hot cheese. "Thanks for the food."

"I haven't seen you around here. You live in one of those mountain mansions?" A man in a Red Bull jacket asked me.

"How do you know?"

"Your car. Not a lot of lifted F-150s around here. They fine you for gas now, unless you're on two wheels."

"Let her eat, Herod."

The name changes are out of control.

They started talking mileage in the booth and I eyed the door. Their bikes were a stubborn display of their commitment to the gas tank. I hate motorcycles. Choosing a motorcycle over a car is like choosing to get punched in the face. I got on and thought about how I'd look facedown on the highway next to a couple fast food wrappers and a mattress. Not so different from how I looked on Gox's messy bed an hour later.

Turns out riding a motorcycle isn't so bad sometimes. Especially at dawn in the country. Not a soul in sight. No weaving through cars at red lights or praying on the highway. Gox dropped me off at my car with his phone number and a promise that he'd call.

*

Charlotte was right. I was losing my mind in the monotony of getting to know the stubbornly shy Daisy and supervising the toddler that had recently discovered running. On the third night, I put them to bed and immediately took the pickup truck back to the bar. Gox wasn't there. Melba was using the slow night to practice monologues. Bill wanted to talk about harvesting adrenochrome. I came home to Bliss and Daisy chewing on Matzah that had expired in 2032.

"That's not food! That's decoration."

A gingerbread house kit was open as well, crumbs and icing all over the carpet.

"You had to go straight for the storage room, Daisy? You couldn't check the fridge or the pantry? I made you three cooked meals. Mac and cheese, meatballs, and mashed potatoes for Bliss. Why?"

   "I forgot."

I cleaned the house, put the girls to bed, and texted Gox to ask if he wanted to come over with something to drink.

He drove up 10 minutes later. I waited for him at the bottom of the hill to make sure his motorcycle wouldn't wake Bliss. He brought a half-drunk bottle of Cuervo that tasted watered down.

*

I laid on the deck listening to the oven ding through two walls and wished one of Charlotte's spawn would turn it off. I heard a man's footsteps and saw Gox pass through the hallway. I didn't know he slept over. I called him over.

"I met your kids this morning. We're making breakfast together."

I closed my eyes and imagined the pile of dirty dishes that was growing with each moment.

"I had this dream you were taking an eyelash out of my eye. The one that grows down, into my cornea, stubborn."

"That was real. You sleep with your eyes open, little white slits, it's creepy. That eyelash bothered me when you're awake. I tried to pry it off with tweezers while you were asleep."

"You had a fucking pair of tweezers in my eye?"

"Yeah. What else was I going to use?"

Bliss started to cry before I could retort.

*

Gox stayed for a few days, making himself at home. I couldn't tell if he was old fashioned, ill mannered, or just a little autistic. But I really craved adult company.

Bliss curled up next to me in her striped pink and gray onesie. Her little towhead was messy and stuck to the pillow via static electricity. She was hot to the touch, so hot that I had to move my arm away. I needed to find the baby aspirin Charlotte's fat husband was supposed to be taking after his heart attack. I looked back at them on the bed together, him deep in his phone.

"Babies fall backwards suddenly. It's what they do."

He ignored me for a dial tone. I heard him use his real name on the phone with a realtor. "Hi, it's Mike again."

"Don't get distracted. Don't relax."

"I am absolutely not relaxed."

"Good."

As I looked through the mirror cabinet something huge and gray entered my periphery. A creature ran through the trees down the neighbor's driveway, barely visible through the bathroom mirror. I got scared for a minute before remembering what a dog is, remembering that people have dogs, that you can just buy one. It's harder to get a job in a drive-thru as a felon than become the owner of a 200 pound canine. Or become a parent. I heard Bliss start crying and rush back into the bedroom.

"I was on the phone, I looked away for one second."

Bliss had fallen off the bed facefirst into the corner of the nightstand. A red welt was forming on her cheek right below her eye.

"Thank god she didn't lose an eye or a tooth. Grab some ice from the kitchen."
   "I need to finish this call."

I took his phone and threw it across the room, through the door, clattering down the staircase.

"Get the fuck out."
   "Whatever. I'll use yours."
   He grabbed my phone off the bed and started to leave the room with it. With Bliss crying on my hip I kicked him down the stairs as he tried to pick his phone up. I ran to the master bedroom and took Keith's handgun out of the drawer.

"Leave. Forget this address."
   "Are you serious?"
   "Get on your bike and go, *Mike*."

As I heard his bike rip away, down the road, I realized he never even asked for my name. Daisy ventured out of the attic while I was watching a video tutorial for a sling you can tie out of an old blouse. I wasn't going to let Bliss out of my sight for a moment.

"What happened?" Daisy asked, hiding her chest with her book. Her shyness was starting to piss me off. I watched it turn to vanity, like a spoon twisting in the light.
"You heard your sister crying and stayed up there, reading?"
   "You're here to take care of us."

"You're twelve fucking years old. You want to be a grownup when you're up late talking to your internet boyfriends but when it comes time to take care of your sister or wash a single dish, suddenly you're a child again."

"At least my internet boyfriends don't *live* here."

"I met him *in person.* And I'm calling your grandma. Yes, *that* grandma. Molly Marie. She's going to pick you up and take you to the farm while your mom's in New York."

*

The second Frank and Molly Marie picked up the girls, I got undressed and peeled off the pool cover. I promised Charlotte I'd keep it closed around Bliss to prevent any Casey Anthony incidents. I fell asleep in the sun and woke up in the back of a car with a hood over my face.

I could feel that I was sitting in the middle of the backseat, falling into the people next to me at turns. Men, by their smell and size and the firmness of their arms. One of them was wearing an acrid, soapy, anise-heavy cologne. The other smelled natural, sweat and unwashed hair. The car smelled like fake purse leather. I wondered if this had something to do with Charlotte's trial.

"Do you think I'm Charlotte Sachs?" I asked, quietly. "I'm Jen. I'm just house sitting."

I heard the men in front talking amongst themselves for a little. One of them ran his hands under my hood and felt my face like a blind man. His hands smelled sweet, like chewing tobacco.

"Where is Charlotte?"

"I don't know. I was just watching her parents' house."

"Her husband? Children? Where are they?"

"Children? She has PCOS."

"I know she has children. There were two girls in the house." I heard a familiar voice coming from the front seat.

"Charlotte became delusional after her second miscarriage. She 'borrowed' two girls from a foster home. She doesn't have any biological kids, just orphans she babysits a little. The girls are back in their home, and Charlotte is in jail. They arrested her for kidnapping."

"You said you didn't know where she was."

"I don't know which jail she's in. She has warrants in multiple states."

I tried to think of a lie they'd believe. Paint a picture. Men aren't familiar with Lifetime Network patter:

What the husband says about his old bag of a wife to get the surrogate to sleep with him,

What the surrogate tells her ex-con boyfriend to get him to kill the husband,

What the wife tells her divorce lawyer.

You know, pillow talk.

We pulled into a place that smelled like gasoline. It could be one of three gas stations in the state. Maybe a truck stop. They talked about the pros and cons of feeding me.

"If we lift your hood you'll see our faces. You get that, right?" One of them patted my knee. They seemed nervous.

"Fill up a jug of gas and let's get out of here."

"How much does your bike take?"

Again, *mileage.*

I smiled under my hood. I started to paint a picture of the car. Gox/ Mike was in the passenger seat. Herod was driving. Dupont Damon was to my right, and Red Bull was to my left. I was strapped in the catbird seat. Gox/Mike was trying to obscure his voice but I heard the nasally lilt men of his generation tend to have. Someone stuck a helmet over my hood. I felt the car lurch dangerously to the left and heard the men start yelling. Five gunshots, two shells bouncing off my helmet. I heard a man breathing heavily, yelling into a phone. A woman's voice on the other end. I felt someone unbuckle my seatbelt and carry me from the car without cutting the zip ties from my wrists. I saw a flash of light through my hood. A camera. I heard him get back into the car, slam the door shut, and start the engine. The sound of the car crashing into something immovable made me fall asleep.

I woke up on Charlotte's couch with sore wrists and a bruise across my chest. Melba was in the kitchen, in Charlotte's bathrobe, slicing strawberries on ice cream. She offered me some with her shoulders and wrists, silently, without interrupting the man speaking. Damon closed the fridge and sat down next to me. They paused like parents with bad news.

"Keith can't go to prison."

"All that skin…" Melba continued.

"They'd keep him alive for less than a year, if he's lucky. They'd hook him to a feeding tube and hack him up."

"What's that got to do with me?"

I got up to go to the bathroom and stared out the window looking for the neighbor's dog. The driveway was empty except for two cars, Melba's sedan and an Organ Transport Vehicle. No white truck.

"The organ transport guy's car battery ran out." Melba's thighs smacked on the toilet cover next to me. "I told him he can charge it here. Poor guy will probably get fired. 30 minutes or it's free right? I heard they used to deliver pizzas with that promise." She was lying, nervous, scratching inside her boot with a pen, waiting for me to answer. "How are you doing? After the crash, I mean."

"Which one?"

I kept watching for the gray dog, wary of how it tended to blend into the neighbor's asphalt driveway as he napped. I heard Melba asking me something about prison. Unearthing the lede.

"Ever wonder why Charlotte called Fauquier County and got you out early?"

"Alderson. Not Fauquier. FCC was the second to last place they sent me."

"Alderson, right. I heard they really shrink wrapped you in there."

"Nothing gets past you."

"Last year Charlotte produced a feature, starring herself, reenacting the whole night you crashed. They were gonna show you that under hypnosis. But the girl who was supposed to play you got injured in the stunt crash. Charlotte paid her off and scrapped the whole thing."

"How badly was she hurt?"

"She's fine. Just a little burnt." Melba pointed to her shiner.

From my standing position I noticed a black holster in Melba's boot. I tried to flick my gaze away in time but she pulled the gun out and told me to get into the shower. She had the same glint in her eye as her retelling of the Mitzy Katchman case. She grabbed towels off the stack and threw them around me in the tub.

"I heard Charlotte had steering wheel size bruising on her chest and thighs. And that she hired you a very expensive psychiatrist. Recovered memories, hypnosis, meditation. I'm not so sure she had to go through the trouble. You seem to be sleeping on your feet."

"Why did Gox kidnap me? Ransom?"

"Mike didn't plan any of this, he just got the layout of the house and a read on you. Char wanted to be kidnapped with the kids. She really didn't think you'd go over her head like that, sending for Molly. That wasn't so good. Being with her kids would have made it more sympathetic, stalling her trial even longer. But I guess it all worked out in the end."

"She got me out of prison early to use me to stage her kidnapping?"

"You were wearing a black hood and Charlotte's clothes. The rest of the group is dead, they didn't know you were a double, they've never seen Charlotte's face, only her car. She never goes to that dive. You know how this all works by now, right? I wonder what they're going to make out of you. You've got *lovely* skin."

Melba's gun was small and I thought of the stolen valor on the left side of her face that wasn't stolen anymore, she earned it, she'd gotten burned. She had skin in the game. She was still on Charlotte's payroll and I didn't know what other fucked up skin she had hiding under her henleys. I remembered Bill's rants and Mitzy Katchman and New Rochelle. I turned on the hot water and ran a hot bath, letting the towels stop up the drain, wondering if this would be the last warmth my skin got to feel premortem. She got frustrated that my ears were underwater and not listening to her monologue. As she reached for the faucet I wrapped her head in the shower curtain like I saw someone do in Delaware and held her face in four inches of water. As I held her head down with my body weight, waiting for stillness, I saw the gray dog jump our fence and run uphill towards the house. I saw Damon go outside to catch it, giving me one good shot out of the bathroom window.

I piled their bodies under plastic Christmas trees, Thanksgiving wreaths, Easter baskets, as-seen-on-TV head massagers, gingerbread houses, Melba's gun, Keith's gun, and all the rest of the junk I could carry out to the backyard. I lit them on fire using a brass menorah and watched the flames grow as I tread water in Charlotte's pool.

Refrigerator Death Index

Truman Hardie stirred dinner with one eye out the window, waiting for his dad's Taurus. His father traveled every week to schools across the mid-Atlantic and Appalachia as a motivational speaker. His slogan was "Why learn the hard way, when you could learn the Hardie way?" He'd cartwheel across stage while telling kids to stay sober, celibate, and out of jail. He was cheaper than D.A.R.E., his speaking fee barely covering gas and a motel, but he loved the mountain drives under those creamsicle sunsets, dyed to confection by the smelters down the valley. His favorite part of the drive was pulling into the parking lot behind his building and looking up at the third floor windows to see his son waving a big spoon covered in red sauce.

He dragged the computer chair over to the kitchen table while he caught up with Truman.

"Renfro, Kentucky," he winced. "High RDI."

Refrigerator Death Index.

"What was their PPQ potential?"

Pregnant Prom Queen.

"Safe bet."

"See any CCCPs in the parking lot?"

Coke Can Crack Pipe. Alternatively, *Carseat Condom Confetti Party.*

"You bet, I even found myself parked next to Jack and Diane. Those neckers would've made John Cougar proud."

They set the table and sat down to join hands, wrists up near the chili pot, locked in a silent Quaker prayer. Cass took a deep breath with his eyes still closed and squeezed his son's hand.

*

It was an unseasonably warm winter day in Maryland and Truman asked his lab partner if she'd like to skip Astronomy and walk to the creek with him. Chiomara had a flat Mayan face, a face carved in stone somewhere below the equator. Wide forehead, high cheekbones, dark eyes. She nodded.

"Ask to go to the bathroom in 15 minutes. I'll be long gone."

He was bad at whispering, but nobody noticed him anyway. Truman was a wiry kid, short for his age, weak chin, a cartoonishly deep voice.

Truman broke off an icicle and started to eat it.

"Don't. They're filthier than they look."
    "Can I call you Chief?"
    "Sure. Why?"
    "You have the face of an Indian Chief, you look powerful, quiet. The stoic type. Your name would be…Dark Horse Crouching Behind a Storm Cloud. Or Mountain Lion Climbing up Concrete."
    "Indians don't have concrete."
    "Of course they do. You think those casinos are made out of leftover wigwams or something?"
    "Your Indian name would be Wet Weasel."
    "Wet Weasel?"
    She pointed to a big brown puddle as Truman stepped into it, soaking his jeans up to his right knee.

"I have to walk home like this," he cursed.
    "My sister can drive you."
    "No thanks. I don't want to meet her covered in mud."

He heard his dad's voice: *First impressions, Tru.*

*

Chiomara's parents, Amy and Robert, worked for the WWF and IMF. They adopted four girls from four different countries: Liberia, Vietnam, Ecuador, and Ukraine. Every night, the housekeeper would send her son to four different restaurants. Amy thought it would be easier on their microbiome and help them adjust to their new lives if each girl ate the cuisine of her ethnic origin. Usually it was soul food for Talia, banh mi for Chloe, burritos for Chiomara, and pierogies for Sasha. They all envied Chiomara.

"We should bribe the delivery boy." Talia picked at the undercooked potatoes in her Jamaican meat pie.

"We could give Gonzalo a bottle from the wine cellar, wrap it up really nicely," Chloe suggested.

"Nah, Robert autistically catalogs his wines for his blog. Besides, it's locked, like the fridge," Sasha reminded her, pouring a small hill of dry curry over her pelmeni.

"Not when he's down there."

"When have you been down there?"

"We could give him a little bit of our allowance and some of my Xanax." Talia finished scraping the filling out of her pie crust and wrapped it up in a napkin.

Chiomara looked down at her tinfoil, uncomfortably full. Ever since the Oaxacan restaurant closed, Gonzalo had been grabbing her Chipotle on his evening runs to get the girls food from four different restaurants. She didn't want to say anything— she saw how much his shoulders ached after his nightly deliveries. She watched him get off his bike in the driveway, weighed down by his huge insulated backpack.

"We shouldn't make trouble for Gonzalo. Amy fired the last two housekeepers over nothing."

"Lidia vacuumed up wet papier-mâché and ruined a Dyson. That's not *nothing.*"

"It's nothing for them. Lidia got fired because she was too pretty. And Maria's a better driver, anyway."

"Why isn't Maria allowed to cook?"

"Amy doesn't like food smells in the house. I tried to microwave a breakfast sandwich last week and she flipped. She doesn't like having any temptations around, no self control. Did you see her housing champagne and hors d'oeuvres at the Library of Congress last week?"

"I wasn't there."

"Right." Sasha blushed and thought of a way to change the subject. Amy had been coming up with excuses to leave Chiomara at home ever since she started gaining weight. She used to love parading the four of them around, feeling like the Angelina Jolie of Potomac. "Maybe we can trade off some nights?"

"No one's gonna want to trade for my dry pickled cabbage sandwiches," Chloe pouted.

*

The girls hung a blanket over the railing that looked out over the dining room and hid behind it, eavesdropping on their parent's dinner party. They passed around a bottle of wine Sasha swiped from the kitchen. Amy was catching up with her best friend from college, Lisa, an immigration lawyer. They were speaking at a drunk volume and the girls barely had to strain to listen.

"It's been three years since we adopted Chiomara. I have the *itch*."

"I can get you a Haitian baby this summer, easy," Lisa stroked Amy's arm. "It's hurricane season."

"Can't they make an earthquake in Denmark, Sweden, or something? A flood, maybe?"

Chloe's stomach rumbled. The smell of crab cakes filled the house.

"Thank god for the Black Student Fund. Not only did we get Talia into Holton Arms, we got a big discount."

Talia's eyes reddened and her face started to puff. Sasha knew there was a five second window before she broke into one of her wailing tantrums. She dragged her into Chloe's bedroom and motioned the other girls in. A knock on the door startled them all. Sasha cracked the door and slipped through. Chloe put her ear up to the paint and listened.

"Miss Amy wants the four of you to put on your matching dresses and come downstairs right now."

"We'll be down soon!"

Sasha ran into the room and started putting concealer on Chloe's Asian flush.

"Finish yourself so I can grab the dresses from Talia and Chiomara's rooms."

The dresses were cheap blue satin, with short sleeves that fell an inch below their shoulders. Chiomara's wouldn't zip in the back and she started to cry. Chloe took a box of safety pins to it but they wouldn't hold. Sasha paced around the room, thinking of a plan.

"Put this shirt on underneath and let your hair down. I'll have my arm around your shoulders so people can't see. We're going to line up on the steps, prom-like. A dramatic entrance, and a quick exit. I'll introduce everybody. If they ask us any questions, or try to make us come down, I'll tell them we have an early soccer practice or something, Amy doesn't remember our schedules anyways. The important thing is Talia stays quiet and nobody sees the back of Chiomara's dress."

Sasha put her hand on her hip and gave the room a Cinderella wave. The red wine was hitting her and she wondered what would happen if she put her fingers down her throat and vomited on her parents, the guests, and the seafood feast below her. There were more caterers than guests in the room, wearing stupid little butler vests. Amy ate half of a crab leg and threw the rest onto a woman holding a tray full of shrimp tails and dirty napkins. She missed her target, or made it, it was hard to tell with how loudly she laughed at the big stain left on the caterer's shirt. She took another sip of wine and started to introduce the girls.

"My eldest, Sasha, is from an orphanage in Lukhansk. They call them boarding schools over there, it's so apologetic. Beautiful children though. Chloe was adopted from Vietnam. Talia, 15, is from Liberia. When she was 12, her school caught on fire and all of the children were evacuated. Miraculously, there was a UN peacekeeping camp nearby, and they airlifted all of the children to Dulles."

*

"Do you want to go to Cotillion with me tomorrow?"

Truman wondered if that was the first full sentence she'd ever spoken to him. Chiomara would have written it on a note, but she forgot how to spell it.

"I'd love to." Truman couldn't wait to text his dad. Cass always lamented not being able to afford golf, boating, and dance lessons; *"gotta learn how to rub elbows, Tru."*

"Ask your dad tonight."

"It's fine. He's in Mystic. Or Norfolk, I don't remember."

"I'll pick you up after school."

Truman waited for Chiomara in the parking lot, holding a plastic box he'd ran six blocks for at lunch. He wrote "For Chief" on top in silver Sharpie. The Lexus SUV was full of girls who looked nothing like each other, driven by a middle aged Latina.

"Is that your mom?"

"Maria's our housekeeper. I'm Chloe, that's Talia, and Sasha in the back."

A mixed girl with big green eyes nodded towards him. A blonde girl who looked 25 was laying across the backseat with big headphones on. The talkative one in the front seat was a pretty Asian girl with long hair and pink braces all over her teeth.

"I'm Truman."

"Did Maria bring snacks?" Sasha pulled her headphones halfway off.

Chloe threw a pack of pretzels over her shoulder. Talia ripped the bag open impatiently, causing a small Chernobyl in the middle seat. She ate her wanton pretzels off Truman's lap without looking, like he was part of the upholstery. Her nails hit the plastic box between his knees.

"Oh my god, is that a corsage?"

"Who's Chief? Is that what he calls you?"

"That's *perfect.* She looks exactly like Sitting Bull."

"Put it on her!" Sasha yelled from the backseat.

"Not until we're inside." Truman had watched three video tutorials on how to tie it around her wrist, and not a single one was filmed inside a moving car.

"What a gentleman." Maria cooed from the driver's seat.

Truman texted his father a picture of himself in the country club's spacious bathroom, a big white lily pinned to his chest.

"Have fun, Tru. I love you."

He put his father's love back into his back pocket and did a few sit-ups on the tiles before a bridesmaid in a yellow dress barged into the bathroom.

"Sorry!" Truman blurted out, hands still folded behind his head.

"It's okay. You're in the right place. I was supposed to meet someone here, but I guess he's late." She hiked her dress up and hopped up on the sink. "Why are you doing sit ups?"

Truman felt no need to lie to the woman pissing in the sink with her feet dangling in front of him. "I read that it would help my stomach stop grumbling. I didn't have time for lunch because I had to go buy a corsage."

"That's sweet." Her hair was styled in spiral curls half in a bun, half waterfalling down her bare shoulders. "Hey, I can get you some food. You're dressed so fancy, you'll fit right in. They'll think you're one of the bride's little cousins." She held her hands out and pulled Truman off the floor.

"I'm Shelly."

"Truman Hardie, nice to meet you."

"That's a hot name. You'll grow into it."

"Is it hot, or have I not grown into it?"

"What are you, 14?" She passed by a pyramid of champagne glasses and pulled four into the crook of her arm like she'd been doing this her whole life. Two of the glasses pushed her left breast up and Truman took one to stop staring. It tasted nothing like his dad said.

"Is there alcohol in this?"

Shelly pulled him into her chest and kissed his forehead. "You're so cute. Have another."

Truman chugged another flute of champagne and wondered how long he'd left Chiomara alone.

"I have to go back."

"No, you have to eat."

"I left her alone at cotillion with her mean sisters. I have to go."

Shelly pulled him back into the hallway and gave him a big wet champagne kiss. Two firsts in five minutes.

A tipsy Truman danced like a flame to Shotakovich in the room full of stiff teenagers. He pulled Chiomara close and whispered compliments into her stud earrings. "You don't look like Sitting Bull. You look like Pocahontas."

"You smell like wine," Sasha whispered in his ear, leaning over the middle seat.

"Champagne, actually." He leaned back and clicked his seatbelt. There was nothing anyone could say to him tonight. He went to bed hungry, but content, thinking about his night. His first kiss with Shelly, Chiomara's cotton candy perfume, her older sister whispering to him, her lips grazing the little elf tip part of his ear.

*

Amy read the newspaper while chewing on a celery stick. *"A 15 year old girl named Aracely Diaz was shot in Wheaton Regional Park. Montgomery County law enforcement suspect MS-13. A special education assistant teacher at Wootton High was arrested with 3 terabytes of child pornography. Benjamin Whitehall had filmed hundreds of sexual assaults on disabled students, some non-verbal…"*

Sasha dropped her fork. "Mom!"

"So? It's important to read these things. It should remind you to be grateful, and appreciate the life we've given you."

"Don't act like you found us in the sewer and knocked the flies off yourself. Sometimes I can't tell if you're oblivious, or just cruel."

Chiomara's shoulders pressed back onto her father's chair at the end of the table. She raised her palm and called Sasha's dogs off. Her older sister's face burned red, wondering what consequences she'd get for her outburst. Amy's clay mask masked any evidence of a reaction.

"Whatever, Sasha. Finish your borscht and go to school."

*

A substitute in gray sweatpants dropped a manila folder on the teacher's desk. Truman and Chiomara gave each other one look before they grabbed their backpacks and left.

The other day Truman had found a big orange cable plugged into the back of the CD/Game Exchange. He followed it into the woods until his dad called him back to the parking lot.

"Let's see where it goes. Maybe there's a secret arcade in the woods."
    The cable continued into the woods, disappearing under a sprinkle of leaves and dirt every twenty feet.

A semicircle of tents curved around a pile of trash, sticks, and a metal barrel. The orange cable continued into the homeless camp. They didn't need to tell each other that it was time to head back.

"I think they saw us," Chiomara said. "Let's change course. Walk back along the creek."

Truman was sweating in his khakis and half zip. He felt shy and stupid that he'd led Chiomara into a homeless camp in pursuit of his Narnia like childish dream. He heard her breathing heavily and offered a break on a nice flat rock along the creek.

A full bottle of Modelo sat upright, the foil still wrapped around its opening. Truman peeled it off and tried to pop the cap off with the edge of a rock. A shard of the neck cut into his palm. He passed it to Chiomara.

"Modelo time?"

She took an air sip, twisting the sharp edge away from her lips. "Have you ever drank before?"

He wondered what she'd think about him sneaking the champagne at Cotillion. She hadn't said a word, but if her sister smelled it from the backseat, Chiomara must have been wise to it as well.

"A couple times. But my dad is really against it. That's his whole life, honestly. Telling kids not to drink and stuff."

"My dad drinks. A lot. He has a whole wine cellar in the basement, with a big leather couch in the middle, a big table cut from a geode, a bearskin rug. He sleeps in there most of the time."
   "How old were you when you were adopted?"
   "Twelve. We were all preteens, Amy doesn't do little kids."
   "I'd hope not," Truman joked. She fell quiet and he felt guilty for making light of her situation. They walked in silence for a ways and Truman wondered what it would be like to grow up in a rich family full of strangers.

"My mom didn't like small children, either. She only had me. I guess I was too much for her."
   "Where is she now?"
   "She died when I was 8."

He thought he heard something over the rustle of their footsteps. "Do you hear voices?"
   "Just yours."
   "I think I hear someone."

A group of men were at the top of the hill. They had a young girl with them.
   "She looks our age. Maybe it's okay?"
   "Run!" Chiomara whispered.
   Truman ran down the hill, trying to follow the orange cable out of the woods. He was reassured by the scattering of leaves behind him, knowing Chief was right on his heels. Until he stopped, and the leaves

stopped. He'd lost her.

He exited the woods and flagged down a cop parked near a liquor store.

"What were you doing in there? There's a damn hobo metropolis in the middle. And lots of MS-13 activity. Rule of thumb, stay away from the woods behind storage units, gas stations, and hardware stores. Lotta illegals sleep in the woods behind Lowe's."

The cop walked at a slow pace, like he was looking for a lost cat. The sun was going down and every bare tree and pile of leaves looked identical. Truman noticed a big white metal box half submerged in the creek. He ran towards it, breaking his wrist as he fell into the cold murky water.

*

Truman was tired of pacing through the hallways in his yellow cast. He was hungry, bored, and terrified of Chiomara's parents. He'd been in the hospital for hours, waiting for his dad to drive back to Maryland. He wrote Chiomara a poem with his bad arm. It took him twenty minutes and he felt stupid and shy.

> *Life is short but you look beautiful in heels*

> Television tip-over,
> Refrigerator death,
> Chiomara gave her husband
> A freshly severed head.

> That Centurion, who had the Gaul,
> He had to learn the hard way,
> That there's love in every slice,
> And with you It's Always Friday.

> PS- can we go to Papa Johns on my birthday?
> PPS- did you know your name means "great in battle?" I looked
> it up on the computer yesterday.

He folded the poem back into his pocket and went to eavesdrop on Chief's hospital room. The older sister who smelled the champagne on his breath was alone in there with her.

"You're the only one who was allowed to keep her real name!" Chiomara cried.

"I wasn't. She tried to start calling me Nicole, and made me take my cross off. She would lock me in my room without food and water, lock the bathroom so I'd piss myself, tell the teachers at school to separate me from the other children. She'd lock me in my room and sit outside the door, drinking and berating me. I could hear the wine glass chink against my doorknob as she screamed through the keyhole. She told me my dad was probably an alcoholic nuclear radiation freak who raped my mom while she was passed out drunk in a snowbank. And maybe she's right. But Amy is just Amy. She's not my mother, just some woman who I have to see for twenty minutes a day until I turn 18."

"Was it hard, being the first, before she adopted the rest of us?"

"It was. But honestly, it's harder for me now. Back then I just felt angry, persecuted, sorry for myself. But now I have you three to worry about. You make it harder to—"

Sasha trailed off, watching a tall blonde man doing cartwheels down the hallway.

"My son is alive!" Cass cried out. "And he's a hero!"

He hugged every nurse in a six foot radius. He hugged Robert and even picked him up a little.

"Isn't a beautiful day to be a dad? Our kids are okay!"

"How did he know to look inside the refrigerator?"

Claw Clip

THE BLOOMINGDALES was dirty and scantly manned by rude women with burnt hair and talc on their black blazers. Powder, dust, and dandruff. They sprayed each other with J'adore and avoided eye contact like lazy students scattering from a teacher. Seagulls on the beach. Karina put her phone down on a greasy glass display to try on a claw clip she liked. Tortoiseshell flanked with mother of pearl. It was lightweight and didn't tug her scalp, which had grown more sensitive since she moved to the East Coast. The hard water came out of the tap smelling like a rain puddle on a rusty roof and ruined her skin and hair.

"*Perlamudre,*" she whispered, knowing her boyfriend was barely paying attention on the other side of the call. She took a photo of her dark hair swept into a messy bun but decided against sending it to him.

"I have to go, I have to pay and go upstairs to meet Bethany."
  "That big blonde girl I met?"
  "She's not so big. You met her right after she had the baby. Be nice."
  "She's the girl with the stillbirth, right? That was bleak."
  "Her husband's so old, I wasn't even surprised. It was a miracle they even got pregnant after 4 cycles of IVF. I can't even imagine how much they spent to get that baby."
  "I grew up on a farm, could've done it for free."
  Karina laughed. "Be nice. I have to go."

She bought the $60 claw clip and went upstairs to the cafe. Bethany was waiting at a table near the window, in baggy sweatpants and an IU sweatshirt. She jumped up for a hug.

"You look great, Karina. Did you just get a facial?"

"Alla Shestopalova. Best fillers in the area. Nobody can tell, people keep thinking I lost weight, or got pregnant." Karina smacked her new lips and pursed them around her straw. She winced when she noticed Bethany's face fall. She kept talking to shove her last words aside. "$200 a pop if you pay cash."

"Ben will make fun of me. He'll call me fish lips."
"Mine don't look fishy." Karina admired her mouth in her compact. "He won't even notice. I'll take you tomorrow after Pilates."
"I'm not going tomorrow."
"Why, you got a job or something?"
"I can't work out right now. Not until I see a doctor."

Bethany's slight pause before *doctor* was a tell. Karina scanned her, noticing the way she could barely sit still on the wooden chair.

"Alla's a doctor."
"I don't need a *cosmetologist.*" Bethany fidgeted, tucking her leg under herself, hovering over the chair.
"You need someone to take a look under your hood?"
"Yes."
"Alla's licensed as a dentist, but can do it all. And very discreetly, at that. I don't go to anyone else."
"Does she take cash?"
"Of course."
"I think Ben is cheating again."
"How? He's so old."

Bethany started to cry in a way that made Karina feel embarrassed but sympathetic. She untied the silk scarf from the handle of her purse and offered it to her.

"Don't use that napkin. The paper will tug at your skin and cause wrinkles."

*

Alla's practice was in a medical plaza five minutes away from the mall. The office smelled clean; soapy and aldehydic from the ambient Chanel and Givenchy perfumes worn by the patients and employees. Mumbles of Russian, Ukrainian, and Hebrew darted across the room. The coffee table was laden with thick glossy magazines, all recent.

The blonde behind the desk greeted Bethany politely, without a smile. The lapels of her white robe were folded down, revealing a perfect pair of breasts of questionable authenticity. *Perks of the job,* Bethany mused.

Alla had a blunt bob, that dark burgundy shade of hairdresser red. She was more thorough than any doctor Bethany had ever been to. She insisted on weighing her patients naked, inspecting her skin, scalp, teeth, eyes, and posture as Bethany tried not to look at the number on the scale. She shined a light into her armpits and between her toes. She felt around Bethany's stomach slowly and rhythmically.

"Povyshennaya davleniye, dermatit, potentsialnaya pochechnaya infektsiya." Alla noted for her nurse to write down. Bethany wished she understood more Russian than *privyet* and the dirty words Karina had taught her. The only thing she caught was the last word. Infection.

"Can we be alone for a moment?"

The nurse turned a heel without needing to be shooed away. Bethany always admired how Russians seemed to taste the air, read minds, fill in the blanks without any ceremonious dialogue, smiling, or sugarcoating. She thought Karina was uniquely telepathic until they traveled to Moscow together.

"My husband has been cheating on me. This is the second time in a year I've come down with something. Last time, I took some leftover antibiotics from his medicine cabinet, and it cleared up in two weeks. I felt embarrassed going to the doctor. But this time, something feels very wrong. I'm in a lot of pain. I had a stillbirth last year..."
   "You want me to do a pelvic exam?"
   "Yes, please."
   "I'll use the small speculum. For shy girls." Alla winked at her.

Bethany scooted to the end of the exam table and slid her feet into the hand-knitted socks covering the stirrups.

"Did you make these?"

"My daughter, when she was nine."

The ceiling was plastered with classical paintings, some she recognized as Bruegel and Kandinsky. One was a portrait of a pale woman combing her long dark hair in the mirror. Her vanity was cluttered with candlesticks, hair pins, perfume bottles, and pearls spilling out of a jewelry box. Her white nightgown was pulled off one shoulder, showing off the lines of her neck and collarbone.

"Which painters do you have up there?"

"Serebriakova, Repin, Vasnetsov, Bruegel, Martynova. Just something to distract you from what I'm doing."

"What do you see?"

"Courbet," Alla joked. "L'origine du Monde."

The speculum clattered on a paper-lined metal tray. A nurse rushed in at the sound and swiped it out of the room. Alla snapped her gloves off and threw them on the tray as the nurse backed out the room.

"What do I have?"

"I won't know exactly until I test your blood, but you have a herpes outbreak in tandem with a pelvic infection. Are you experiencing nerve pain?"

Bethany closed her legs and started to sob on the exam table.

"Tell me more about your husband."

"When will the blood test be ready?"

"I'll call you."

*

The music was too quiet in Saks. Bethany pulled Karina into a rack of sequined prom dresses to whisper her diagnosis.

"Alla just called. She said I let it go untreated for too long and now I have a kidney infection on top of everything else."

"What time do you have to be in her office today? I'll come with you." Bethany was fidgeting conspicuously in the waiting room. Karina took her claw clip out and fixed it into her hair so she'd stop snapping off split ends and flicking them onto the carpet.

Alla and Karina batted terse Russian phrases to each other over Bethany's head, which Karina was stroking with her long, coffin-shaped nails.

"You don't have to do that, if you don't want to, I know have really bad dandruff right now. Alla said I have dermatitis."
    "I don't seen any flakes," Karina lied.

In high school, Karina won a scholarship for an exchange program between Indiana and Kazan. Her host parents, Martin and Cheryl, gave her a warm Hoosier welcome. Their only child, Bethany, was over the moon about her new roommate, the most exciting thing in Columbus since the pork tenderloin sandwich. They both went to IU and moved to the East Coast together.

"Take the entire course of antibiotics. No alcohol, sugar, bread, or sex. Keep your feet and torso warm at all times. Exercise if you can."

Alla and Karina switched back to Russian. Their tones dropped lower, quicker, harsher. Alla handed her a small paper bag before they left.

"What did she give you?"
    "Steroids, for the swelling in my lips."
    "Your lips don't look swollen."
    "I'll be prepared if they do."

*

Ben was surprised to see Karina knocking on the side door. She waited at the French doors that opened into their spacious granite kitchen.

"*Privyet, krasavitsa.* Don't you girls still go to Pilates together? Beth just left."
    "She forgot to bring a scrunchie. I offered to grab one on my way."
    "Her car is full of them, they're all over the carpets, cupholders, under the seats. Every square inch of the house, too. Take your pick." He pointed to a little slinky-shaped pile of hair ties on the granite island.

"She needs a specific one for working out. It's like, a sports bra, for your ponytail."

"I wouldn't know," he held his hands up and shrugged.

"Of course not. Would you mind checking her bathroom? I don't want to go snooping around without her here."

"Go ahead, she won't mind."

"I can't walk upstairs in my heels. I'll trip on the carpet."

"Why are you wearing heels to the gym?"

"I like to change when I get there. Don't want to be seen wearing sneakers in public. It's a hot pink elastic with a blue stripe."

Ben breathed heavily as he trudged up Bethany's room. Karina helped herself to the fridge and poured two drinks with a squeeze of lemon.

"Vodka?" he asked, steadying himself on the granite. "I couldn't find anything hot pink on her bathroom counter."

She rolled her eyes. "It's wine. And thanks for checking."

"Cheers?" he raised an eyebrow, surprised but pleased.

"That's the idea."

She finished her first glass of wine, throwing it back, cooing over him as he showed off his Russian. Ben's Russian always made her squirm. His grammar was too good for a man who had never set foot outside of the US, but his intonation was clumsy, unstressed syllables coming out of his mouth with too much desperation, while the stressed ones stayed back on the diving board, his big purple tongue. State Department, military Russian. The product of two intensive years of studying in Monterey.

His face was becoming a pallid blue. His neck was bent at an unnatural angle against the bottom of the dishwasher. Karina balanced one of her feet squarely between his shoulderblades as she washed the wine glasses, swirling hot, soapy water in the sink. She wondered if he ever used to pay girls to walk on his back in heels. Maybe more than one at a time, there was plenty of room. His obese corpse took up half the kitchen floor. She dried the glasses and put them back on the shelf next to the champagne flutes. She didn't bother checking the kitchen for any other loose ends or wiping prints. She'd been at Bethany's hundreds of times. Karina crossed herself, said a prayer, and drove to Pilates.

*

Sarah parked her ambulance in the bike lane in front of the Korean buffet. As she was pulling in, she heard muffled yelling through the windshield. Somewhere in her peripheral vision, she saw something lime green, black, and angry. A skinny man in full cycling gear was waving his fist at her as he dragged his bike down the right lane. He kept pointing to the GoPro attached to his helmet. He walked around the ambulance with his head cocked, recording all the identifying numbers and text he could find. He jumped around like an agitated mantis, trying to get her attention. She hopped out onto the street.

"Tucker and I just lifted a 300-pound cadaver onto a stretcher an hour ago, some guy who had a heart attack in his kitchen. 300 pounds! Just the two of us. You know how hard that is? I barely weigh 140. Right now, I just want to enjoy my birthday dinner. Film us all you want, I don't give a fuck. Take it up with the county."

The cyclist flipped her off for good measure and biked away.

"He could have at least wished you a happy birthday," Tucker said, holding the door open to Kangnam Palace.

The smell of beef, gochujang, and sesame oil filled her with relief. She slid into the booth where her friends were waiting for her, amazed that they'd ordered ahead.

"I've been thinking about this all day."
    "Surprised that last call didn't kill your appetite."
    "I'm used to it."
    "What a beautiful house," Tucker said, reaching for a dumpling. "Must have been loaded."
    "Speaking of which," Sarah whispered, "I did something bad."

She felt around in her jacket pocket and pulled out a claw clip she found lying on the granite island at their last house. She snapped it open and shut, clicking it in his ear. She pulled her hair away from her face, secured it with the clip, and tucked a napkin into her collar.

Acknowledgments

Tom— without your encouragement, guidance, and faith, my writing would have never left the chamber. Thank you forever.

Will, thank you for your avian eye, wisdom, patience, and tireless effort.

Mark, I have always been an admirer of the BRUISER artwork, and it was a huge honor to have you design the cover of Incurable Graphomania. Thank you so much for lending your talents, genius, and patience.

Thank you to everyone at Apocalypse Confidential, Tragickal, Hobart, Maximus, Expat, and Road Dog Books for believing in my work.

Larry, thank you for purring at my feet as I typed.

Lastly, to all the *graphomans*, I hope you never find a cure.

A Note on the Text.

First, my infinite thanks to Mark Wadley, for his saintlike patience and vision.

This book is set in Caslon, named for the British typefounder William Caslon I. His types were distributed throughout the British empire, and in a wonderful irony, used to print broadside editions of the U.S. Declaration of Independence.

The style and design of this book is loosely based on the beautiful specimen Selected Essays of William Carlos Williams *published in 1954 by Random House. The designer of that book was the great Ernst Reichl, whose influence lives on in this text and many others. Some of his works are available online and can also be found at the Columbia University Rare Book and Manuscript Library. If you ever again see the owl in the folds, say hello for me.*

Ernst Reichl : 1900 - 1980 : R.I.P.

-WW

APOCALYPSE CONFIDENTIAL IS

Jacob Everett...*Publisher & Editor-in-Chief*

Brendan McCauley...*Visual Arts Editor*

Max Thrax...*Managing Editor*

Tom Will..*Poetry Editor*

D.A. Wohler...*Fiction Editor*

Eitan Zion...*Essays Editor*

Tully K..*Editor at Large*

Rachael Haigh..*Director of Operations*

Will Waltz..*Books Editor*

www.ingramcontent.com/pod-product-compliance
Lightning Source LLC
Chambersburg PA
CBHW060455300726
48975CB00008B/2522